Enchant Me:
Brie's Submission #10

By
Red Phoenix

Edited by Mary Yakovets,
Proofed by Becki Wyer & Marilyn Cooper
Formatted by BB eBooks
Cover by CopperLynn
Phoenix symbol by Nicole Delfs
* Special Lea joke provided by Dani Glover

Adult Reading Material (18+)

Dedication

MrRed - my fantasy, my reality

To Brandi, who not only created these covers, but has been my dear friend for years! Thank you for believing in me and my stories—it all started with Blissfully Undone…

To Becki, I remember you were the VERY first one to make an "I googled it, Sir" shirt. You have remained my good friend and dedicated proofer all these years. Hugs!

To Marilyn, you wowed me with your Brie art, then won over my heart. Thank you for your friendship, enthusiasm and creativity.

A special thankyou to all my fans who have followed Brie's journey with me!

CONTENTS

The Honeymoon Begins...

B rie woke up slowly, the pleasant fog of sleep quickly clearing as a sense of excitement took over. She opened her eyes and gazed on Sir as he slept; he had a peaceful expression on his face. Brie had always felt she could see a hint of the young boy he'd once been when the worries of the world weren't reflected on his face.

"My husband..." she whispered.

Her soft words were enough to wake him. She held her breath as those soulful eyes opened and focused on her.

"Wife."

Brie smiled, thrilled that she now carried that title.

"Come here," he commanded with a low growl, pulling her closer to him. "I want to start our first full day as man and wife filling you with my manly essence."

Her insides did a flip-flop, remembering the passion and excitement of being taken without any barriers between them—chemical or physical—the night before.

"How would you like me to make love to you this time?" he asked, rubbing his hard shaft against her.

Brie blushed when she answered, "I'd like to do it missionary style again."

He stopped moving and looked her in the eye, asking in a serious tone, "You're not turning vanilla on me now that we're married, are you?"

"No," she giggled softly. "I just like looking into your eyes when you come inside me."

Sir's growl was husky, his eyes lustful when he answered, "You should not say that or our session will end up unsatisfyingly short."

He left the four-poster marriage bed and returned to her minutes later wearing a wicked grin. "Before we begin, I want to feel the passion of your lips."

Brie smiled, eager to please him that way. When he joined her back on the bed, she took his princely shaft in her hand and lowered her head. "I have always loved this cock," she mumbled seductively.

"It has always loved you," he replied, pushing her mouth toward the head of his shaft.

Brie opened her lips, gratefully encasing his manhood with their soft caress. He tasted of fresh soap, but still retained the manly musk that was uniquely him.

She moaned as she licked the charming head of his cock, tasting the tanginess of his pre-come, excited because his masculine essence now had the power to make a baby inside her. The thought of it sent delightful chills through Brie's body.

She pushed his shaft slowly down her throat as Sir lay back on the bed, sighing in contentment. Unlike most men, he could take the attention of her mouth for over an hour without orgasming. It seemed that the sexual stimulation was relaxing for him, rather than being overly arousing.

It made the experience much more than a simple physical connection; it was a spiritual melding, which Brie cherished. However, in her enthusiasm she lavished too much adoration on his cock. He placed his hand on her head and commanded, "Slow down, wife."

She looked up at Sir, his cock between her lips and smiled apologetically. She knew better; he'd taught her how he preferred it. Thankfully, her Master understood that her excitement over their recent nuptials was the cause for her forgetting the basics.

Brie slowed *way* down, concentrating on the smoothness of the head of his hard shaft, the delicious ridge that she lovingly caressed with her tongue—the feel of it thrilling her in a way he would never know. Then there was the frenulum, which she thoroughly enjoyed licking and teasing.

Whenever Sir allowed her to perform oral pleasures, it gave her the chance to possess his manhood in a way that was as powerful as it was sexy. His cock became her vessel to bestow all her love and affection.

She communicated the gift of her submission, the joy of being his only, and the deep respect she held for Sir not only as her Master, but as her soulmate and husband.

Just as she had been trained at The Center, Brie remembered to voice her pleasure verbally—a flaw she'd been called on early in her training, but rarely suffered from now. She also snuck glances at him as she pleasured him, gratified when she caught Sir staring at her.

The look in his eyes was not only laced with desire,

but with intense love.

Sir's love melted her heart. He could have any woman in the world and yet he had chosen her despite having to lose his position at the center while enduring the financial hit his business suffered after the release of her BDSM documentary. The biggest hurdle of all—Sir never wanted to marry or have children.

This man had overcome so much personally to take her as his wife, and he'd managed the wedding with extreme style and just the right amount of romance. She lifted her head from his shaft and purred, "I love you, Thane."

He smiled down at Brie, his eyes reflecting his building desire. "I think it's time…"

Sir pulled her up to him and lightly caressed her stomach. "I thought last night was the most erotic experience I'd ever had—and that's saying a lot, woman."

She looked at him, biting her lip, and confessed, "I was afraid I might burst into flames because of the intensity of your lovemaking."

"Are you ready to be burned again?" he asked, lifting himself to lay between her legs.

Brie said nothing, gazing into his eyes. How could making a child together be so extremely hot? She'd spent her whole adult life actively avoiding pregnancy, making it seem almost sinful to be engaging in the act now.

"Oh Sir…" she cried as his cock breached her opening and he slid deep inside her.

Instead of thrusting, he remained still. Gazing deep into her eyes, Sir declared, "I don't think a man has loved a woman as much as I love you."

Brie continued to look up at him while he stroked her with his shaft. In silent homage, she wrapped her legs around his waist to pull him even deeper into her.

Sir groaned loudly. "I should *not* be ready to come yet. Have you placed a spell on me?"

Brie smiled. "The spell is of your own creation, husband."

He shook his head, his brow furrowing in frustration. "It seems I have no restraint this morning."

"Come for me then," Brie purred, longing to feel the caress of his seed deep within her.

He grabbed her ass with both hands and grunted as he repeatedly drove his cock home, his whole body shuddering as he orgasmed.

Brie was turned on by the knowledge that he was as desperate for the connection as she was. This was not the serious, controlled Dom she had grown to know and love. This was a groom infatuated with his new bride. It was as if a whole new world had opened up for them to explore together.

After his final thrust, Sir pulled out and lay beside her. "The only positive to a short session is that it allows me to fuck you again that much sooner."

"You'll hear no complaints from me," Brie replied as she caressed his manly jaw. "*The more, the better* as my dad always says."

Sir pretended to hold up an imaginary phone to his ear. "Yes, Mr. Bennett, I'm giving it to your beautiful daughter every chance I get. No sir, I'm not shirking in my duty. The more, the better...until she's unable to walk." Sir winked at Brie. "I promise not to fail in my duty."

Brie laughed. "You're so evil!"

He grinned. "We both know he's trying not to think about what's happening to his precious daughter right now. Should make breakfast interesting…"

"So we're having breakfast with them?" Brie asked in surprise, thrilled at the news.

He pushed back a stray strand of hair, tucking it behind her ear. "Yes, I thought it would be fitting since we head out today. This will be your chance to say good-bye."

"Where are we going, Sir?"

Sir only smirked, shaking his head in answer.

"You're as cruel a husband as you are a Master."

"At least you knew what you were getting into."

Brie smiled as she snuggled up against him. "I did, and I've never once regretted it."

Sir kissed the top of her head. "Shall we go share breakfast with your parents as my come slowly soaks your fresh panties?"

It was Brie's turn to shake her head as she tsked. "Evil to the core."

"Dark and twisted, I'm afraid," he agreed with a grin.

Teasing the Parents

S ir led Brie down the stairs and through the secret corridors of the castle to a fancy dining room. As soon as they entered through the hidden door, Brie was greeted with enthusiastic applause and was tickled to see her friends already seated for breakfast.

Sir guided her to the center table where her parents and Mr. and Mrs. Reynolds were waiting anxiously for them.

"Mom!" Brie cried as her mother stood and gave her a tight hug.

Sir held out his hand to her father and said, "Good morning, Dad."

Her father took his hand and then pulled him closer, giving him a heartfelt but awkward pat on the back. "Yes, good morning to you both."

Sir then turned to Mr. Reynolds. "Unc, it's good to see you this morning."

"Likewise, Thane. You're looking well rested, considering…"

Brie's father cleared his throat, and she had to hide

her smile.

When all were seated, the wait staff brought the six of them a meal of simple, mildly sweet Italian pastries, local fruit, and thin slices of various meats. It was a delightful combination. Brie picked up a small pastry and stared at it hungrily. Just as she was about to consume it, her eyes were covered and she felt large boobs press against her shoulders.

"Guess who?" a familiar female voice sang out.

"Mary?" Brie teased.

"No, silly! It's me." Lea leaned over and whispered, "Dang it, girl. You were positively glowing when you entered the room. Are you already pregnant?"

Brie's father perked up, having heard the tail end of Lea's comment and audibly groaned.

Rytsar strolled up to the group, slapping Sir hard on the back. "*Moy droog*, I trust you made it count last night."

Leave it to the Russian to add fuel to the fire.

Brie felt the trickle of Sir's come between her legs and glanced at him, blushing heavily as she wiggled in her seat.

He winked, knowing exactly what her movement meant.

"Don't tell me you're trying to get her pregnant already," Brie's father said, staring at Sir sternly. "She's just a child herself. Surely you plan on giving her time to live a little before you make her barefoot and pregnant?"

In an uncharacteristic move, her mother took her dad's hand and squeezed it. "Dear heart, this is none of our business. Thane and Brie are married now. They're allowed to do whatever they want with their lives." She smiled sweetly as she reminded him, "We had Brianna not that long after we got married…remember?"

Brie's father snarled, but grabbed a piece of meat and chomped on it to avoid making another comment.

"*Radost moya*, I agree with Ms. Taylor. You do look particularly radiant today."

He turned his attention back on Sir. "If you should need anything—*anything* at all—I am here for you, *moy droog*."

Brie knew exactly what Rytsar was hinting at.

"Rest assured, old friend, I have things under control. We'll be leaving after breakfast to start the formal honeymoon."

"Where are you going, Brie?" Lea asked with interest.

Brie looked at Sir and grinned as she shook her head. "Once again, I have no idea."

Her father frowned. "Really, Thane, this is too much. First, you keep the wedding destination from her, and now the honeymoon too? Are you that much of a control freak…*son?*"

"It's not like that, Dad," Brie protested. "I lost a bet, so I agreed he gets to choose the honeymoon location."

Her mother, trying to defuse the situation, asked playfully, "What kind of bet, sweetheart?"

Brie looked over at Sir with an embarrassed smile, unsure how to explain their aphrodisiac challenge. Before she could utter a word her father barked, "Forget it. We don't want to know."

Mrs. Reynolds piped in, "I'm sure whatever Thane has planned is going to be lovely."

Brie wrapped her arm around her husband's and purred, "I'm sure of it."

Seeing how uncomfortable her father was, Sir steered the conversation away from the current topic, choosing instead to comment on the history of the castle. It proved an agreeable distraction.

But while he talked, Sir snuck his hand under the table so he could rub Brie's wet panties with his middle finger. It took everything in her not to react.

Evil, evil man...

Before Brie left to start their honeymoon, she made it a point to stop at every table to say her good-byes, grateful for every person who had come to be a part of their big day.

She smiled as she walked up to Master Anderson's full table, crammed with Italian women who'd seen him catch the garter from the night before.

"I see you're not starved for company," she teased.

Master Anderson flashed a charming grin. "No, I'm not, and I plan to sample as much Italian cuisine as I can before I return to America." He looked the women over with a lustful eye and the table twittered in delight.

Brie smiled. "Maybe 'the one' is here at this table."

He shrugged with a chuckle. "Who knows?"

"So will you be in LA when we return from our honeymoon?"

"That's the plan."

"Great, then we can meet for dinner and catch up."

"It would be a pleasure, young Brie. I look forward to hearing about your adventures."

She winked at him. "As will I yours..."

Brie moved over to the next table with Baron, Captain, and Candy. "How long are you guys planning on staying in Italy?"

Baron and Captain glanced at each other before Baron answered. "Two more days and then we head back to begin laying down the foundation for a new project."

Brie slid into an empty chair, curious to hear more. "What kind of project?"

Again the two men looked at each other, but this time Captain answered. "It's too soon to say yet, Mrs. Davis, but it's something that Baron and I are both passionate about."

"And me," Candy piped in.

Captain put his hand on hers and nodded. "Yes, pet."

He turned to Brie again. "The three of us share the same vision, but we didn't realize it until we had a chance to talk last night during the reception."

Brie clasped her hands to her chest in excitement. "I can only imagine what it might be, but with the three of you involved it's certain to be a success."

"One can only hope," Baron replied in a deep, mysterious tone. "I was serious when I asked you and Sir Davis to visit my home on your return. We should have much to discuss by then."

"Oh my, you have my curiosity running rampant now," Brie confessed.

Candy's eyes sparkled when she told Brie, "I can't wait to share it with you!"

Captain cautioned, "Until we have things in place, it's best not to speak of it."

"I understand," Brie answered respectfully, even though she was dying to know more. "I'd better continue to make the rounds."

"Yes," Baron agreed. "I know several people who are anxious to speak to you." He nodded towards Tono and Autumn, who were sitting at the next table.

Brie politely excused herself and made her way over to them. "How was your dance?" she asked, sitting beside Tono.

Autumn blushed. "I can't believe you guilted me onto the floor, Brie."

Brie raised her eyebrow. "So you *did* dance."

The grin on Autumn's lips let Brie know it had been a welcomed challenge.

Tono smiled as well. "Autumn is graceful on the dance floor, despite her many reservations."

Shaking her head, Autumn replied, "The only thing graceful about me was you."

Brie chuckled. "Yes, I do remember the first time Tono and I danced together. I only had to look in his eyes and follow his lead to feel confident on the dance floor."

"That's exactly what I experienced last night," Autumn agreed, looking at Tono shyly. "Ren's a wonderful dancer."

"It takes the right partner, Autumn," Tono insisted.

Brie was filled with joy. It was easy to see the attraction the two had for each other. "So will you be staying or heading back to the States right away?"

When Tono glanced at Brie, she was captivated by the feeling of serenity radiating from him. "We agreed it would be good to stay for a week and explore this country. There is much history and culture to be found here. It'd be a shame to miss an opportunity to enjoy it."

"Italy is beautiful, isn't it?" Brie agreed. "Sir has introduced me to a few of his favorite places, but there's still so much to see. I think I'm falling in love with Italy."

"Hopefully your husband won't get jealous," Autumn teased.

Brie giggled, whispering. "I think he's already in love with her, so it'll kinda be a threesome for us."

Autumn blushed, joining in her giggles.

Tono smiled, obviously enjoying the interaction between them. "So where you are headed for your honeymoon, Mrs. Davis?"

Brie loved her new title; it was so much sexier than plain old Miss Bennett. "Truthfully I have no idea. My husband has been as mysterious about the honeymoon as he was about the wedding."

Autumn smiled. "Mr. Davis does like to surprise you…"

"He enjoys keeping her on her toes," Tono explained to Autumn. Returning his gaze to Brie, he added, "You surprised him at the Collaring Ceremony and I believe he remains bound and determined to repay you for that. I don't believe a single person there expected your choice that night."

Brie looked into Tono's chocolate brown eyes, feeling a twinge of guilt. Even though the two of them had moved on since the Collaring Ceremony, she couldn't help wondering if her wedding had rekindled the pain he'd felt that night.

"It's clear you two were fated," Tono assured Brie with a gentle smile.

She reached out, touching his hand, no words necessary.

Autumn glanced from Tono to Brie with a look of concern. For the first time, Brie sensed jealousy coming from her friend and she immediately put both hands in her lap. Autumn's reaction surprised her, but it also hinted to the depth of feeling Autumn had for Tono—and that pleased Brie.

She stood up and gave Autumn a quick kiss on the cheek, whispering, "Have fun in Italy together."

Bowing formally to Tono, she stated, "May you find your heart's desire during your travels."

A slight blush colored his cheeks. "Thank you, Mrs. Davis. I'm certain our travels will be enlightening."

Brie left the couple to seek out Rytsar and found Lea happily chatting away with him at a crowded table.

"Mind if I break in?" she asked the two.

"Not at all, *radost moya*. May I offer you my lap?" the Russian asked, gesturing to his muscular thighs when he noticed there was no place for her to sit.

"Thank you, but I'm sure today will be full of travel, so it's better I stand while I have the chance."

"Very well," he stated, getting up. "I shall stand beside you."

"Me too, girlfriend!" Lea squealed, standing up to Brie to give her a hug. "Did you work things out with your dad? He seemed a little upset."

"We calmed him down," Brie said, raising an eyebrow at Rytsar. "No thanks to you."

He put his hand over his heart. "What did I do that was so wrong? I only wanted to know if my wish to become a *dyadya* was now a reality."

"But in front of my dad?" Brie cried.

"Isn't your father aware of what happens on the wedding night?" Rytsar teased.

"Of course he is. He just doesn't want to think about it. I'm sure you would be the same with your own daughter."

"My daughter would be a nun so I wouldn't have to worry about it."

"A nun?" Brie scoffed.

"But I can see your point," he conceded, putting his hand on Brie's belly. "When tiny *radost moya* is ready to marry, I will not want to dwell on it." He looked up at her with his hand still resting on her stomach. "Should I go apologize to your father?"

"Oh goodness, no!" she giggled. "You'll only make things worse by bringing it up."

When Rytsar removed his hand, he said in a low voice, "Married life agrees with you."

Brie blushed and opened her mouth to agree when she was interrupted by a hip bump from Lea. "So Brie, the next time we see each other I'll either be collared or living in LA."

Brie glanced nervously at Rytsar, wishing Lea hadn't mentioned it in front of him.

"Collared by whom?" Rytsar asked with genuine interest.

Lea realized her mistake too late, and for the first time ever in Brie's experience, Lea was at a total loss for words. No crazy-lame joke came from her lips to cover her oversight.

"Are you hoping to return to Russia with me?" Rytsar asked jokingly. A wicked smile played on his lips as he trailed his finger over Lea's throat. "I have yet to introduce you to my cat o' nines, Ms. Taylor. Shall we head down to the castle dungeon and see how it suits you?"

Lea's eyes widened, a flush coloring her ample chest.

"I see the idea excites you." Rytsar purred like a predatory cat. "Come with me and we can test your limits…"

Brie wondered what it would be like for Lea to experience the allure of Rytsar's sadistic dominance. Surely, Lea must wonder about the magic he possessed that still had a hold over Ms. Clark.

"Although I'm curious…." she began.

Rytsar bit down on her shoulder lightly.

"I can't," she gasped.

"But you can," he insisted.

Lea looked to Brie for help, but closed her eyes in ecstasy when he bit down on her other shoulder.

"Come, Ms. Taylor. Let's play."

Lea leaned over and whispered to Brie, "Please don't say anything," before following Rytsar out of the room as if under a spell.

Brie was stunned. *Lea and Rytsar?* She shook her head, not wanting to think about the possible consequences of such a union.

Mary came up behind her. "Did I really just see that?"

"You didn't see anything," Brie asserted.

"I most certainly *did*." Mary smiled to herself. "Way to go, Lea…"

"Keep it to yourself. Don't even tell Todd. Lea doesn't need Ms. Clark finding out."

Mary folded her arms. "I'm not about to rat her out, but you, Miss Goodie-Two-Shoes? I wonder if you'll be able to keep it to yourself when you see the Domme again."

Wanting to change the subject, Brie asked her, "When are you heading back?"

"Tonight."

"Wow, that's a quick turnaround." Brie spontaneously gave Mary a hug, understanding the sacrifice she'd made in doing such a quick trip.

Mary accepted the physical contact, but responded in typical Blonde Nemesis fashion. "Anything for you, stinky cheese. Well, actually no. I would *not* do anything for you, bitch. I reserve that only for Faelan."

Brie shook her head. "Always the charmer."

Mary shrugged. "No reason to flatter you. We're already friends."

"You sure about that?" Brie teased.

"Better get the rest of your good-byes over with, woman. Looks like your husband is anxious to go."

Brie's heart skipped a beat hearing Mary call him her husband. She looked over to Sir and caught him glancing at her while having an intimate conversation with Marquis. She turned back to Mary and hugged her one last time. "Even though you totally lack social skills, I'm so glad we're friends. Safe travels."

"You too, bitch. Enjoy your vanilla honeymoon."

Brie smiled demurely. "I doubt very much anything associated with Sir will be vanilla."

Mary shook her head. "Still can't believe he agreed to marry you. Most shocking thing I've ever seen."

"Jealous?"

"Not one stinking bit. Marriage is the death of relationships. The clock is already ticking. I give you a year—two years tops."

Brie frowned. "I take it back. I'm not glad we're friends."

Mary shrugged. "Truth hurts, baby. But I'm too much of a friend to lie to your face."

"Please give Mr. Wallace an extra hug from me when you see him tomorrow. I don't think he has any idea what he's gotten himself into by collaring you."

Mary only laughed as she headed over to Captain and Candy's table.

Brie sighed in exasperation, but her resentment quickly died when she walked over to join Sir.

"Are you almost ready, babygirl?" he asked, putting his hand around her waist possessively.

"I am." She looked up at Sir, bursting with love for the man.

Celestia gave Brie a quick squeeze. "Yesterday was magical, from the ceremony and the reception to the luxurious accommodations. Everything has been something to cherish and remember. Truly a blessing to be a part of this important moment in your life."

"You are so sweet to say that," Brie replied, thinking back on Mary's unkind assessment and shaking her head in amusement.

Marquis stated, "There is something sacred about making vows before God with friends and family present." Marquis looked at Sir. "Even when you are still unsure of His existence."

Sir nodded. "I'll concede there may be a God, Gray. However, I would honor my vows regardless."

"As would I," Brie agreed. "Still, I cherish the vows we said to each other, as well as what you added, Marquis. It was perfect. I couldn't be happier."

Celestia bowed to Marquis. "I was so deeply moved by your wise words, Master. It is an honor to be your collared submissive."

Marquis gave a rare smile as he took his sub's hand and kissed it. "The honor is mine, Celestia."

The romance between them was moving and reminded Brie of the night when the two had come to her aid at the Collaring Ceremony. They were a powerful couple who had a tremendous influence over the community.

"Gray, thank you again for officiating the wedding."

Marquis stared intensely into Sir's eyes before replying. "I know it was difficult for you to ask. You and I do not have an easy history, but the esteem I hold for you is real and continues to grow."

Marquis looked at Brie, his gaze becoming tender. "It is rare to find a couple so well matched. I doubted it once, but I can see now I was wrong."

Sir immediately corrected him. "You were not wrong, and were justified in calling me out on several occasions. It acted as an unwanted, but needed motivator."

"It is my nature to demand people live up to their potential."

"Not an easy thing to do, but I'm glad you continually challenge me," Celestia said, looking at Marquis with pride.

He kissed her on the forehead. "Your grace under pressure is inspiring, my sub. It takes an exceptional woman to partner with someone as uncompromising as me."

Brie piped in, "Yes, because you are all kinds of scary intensity."

He gave Brie the barest of smiles. "My gift to the world."

Sir squeezed Brie, letting her know it was time to go. "We will talk again, Gray. Once we return home."

"Sounds good, Sir Davis."

"Safe flight," Brie called out as Sir escorted her toward the door. Marquis nodded as Celestia waved goodbye.

First Destination

"**B**efore we leave I'd like to say good-bye to my grandparents," Sir informed Brie.

"Of course," she replied, glancing around the room. "Where are they, Sir?"

"My grandmother adores roses. I suspect we'll find them in the garden."

Brie touched the special pin on her blouse. "I hope she knows how much this heirloom means to me."

Sir smiled as he looked down at the blue stone. "It's part of the reason I want to speak to them today."

The two walked out onto the large terrace that looked over the labyrinth of roses down below.

"It's truly breathtaking," Brie said in awe as they walked down the stone steps.

The air surrounding the garden was filled with the sweet fragrance of the rose blossoms. "The scent of roses makes me think of you, Sir."

"Does it, Mrs. Davis?" he said with a knowing smile.

"That day you used rose petals as my blindfold and then challenged me not to move is a day I will never forget."

He gently patted her hand, which was resting on his forearm. "Ah, yes. That was a worthy lesson."

"It has helped me on several occasions since."

He looked up, smiling to himself. "I trusted it would."

She squeezed his arm lovingly. "Oh my goodness, what will the next fifty years hold?"

Sir chuckled as he raised his hand to wave at his grandfather, who was standing next to a bench beside Nonna and Aunt Fortuna.

"*Nonna*," Sir said, helping his grandmother to her feet so he could hug her. She stopped him, staring into Sir's eyes with a look of love and something more...

Possibly sorrow? Brie wondered.

Nonna was slow to speak, her voice laced with emotion. The two exchanged words Brie was not familiar with, but the tone let her know it must be something to do with Sir's father.

Sir said nothing as he wrapped his arms around the tiny woman and held her tight. Aunt Fortuna started crying and Brie had to hold back the tears that threatened in her own eyes.

His grandfather broke the tearful moment by clapping his hands together and commanding, "*Niente lacrime.*"

His grandmother nodded as Aunt Fortuna quickly dabbed her eyes with a hanky. Brie had to assume he'd said "no crying" because both women held the remaining tears back.

Nonna smiled at Sir, patting his cheek lovingly. "*Pro-*

prio come tuo padre."

Sir explained to Brie in a hoarse whisper, "She says I am like my father."

Brie echoed his grandmother's smile, not trusting herself to speak.

A flow of beautiful Italian words followed as Sir pointed to the pin on Brie's blouse. Nonna only listened, a knowing smile playing on her lips as he spoke. She gave him a peck on the cheek and then turned to face Brie.

"*La mia belle nipotina.*"

Brie lit up knowing that Nonna had called her "beautiful granddaughter". When they hugged, she noticed a marked difference in the embrace. For the first time, it felt as if she had been a part of this family for generations. Tears ran down Brie's cheeks as the feeling of total acceptance overwhelmed her.

"*Niente lacrime,*" Nonno insisted again.

Brie suddenly realized he was telling *her* not to cry and dutifully wiped the tears away.

Sir's grandfather then held out his arms and Brie gratefully rushed into them. His masculine scent reminded her of Sir and made her love him all that much more. While he held her, he spoke to Sir in Italian, his deep voice causing vibrations in his chest that Brie could feel against her cheek. It caused her to sigh in contentment.

Like grandfather, like grandson.

The two continued to talk, his grandfather still holding Brie tight. When he released her, he put her hand in Sir's, saying solemnly, "*Prenditi cura di lui.*"

The grandfather placed his gnarled hand on both of

theirs and looked at Sir, stating in the same tone, *"Prenditi cura di lei."*

Brie glanced at Sir with a questioning look.

"Nonno told both of us to take care of each other," Sir answered, his voice gruff with emotion.

Brie put her other hand on top of his grandfather's and vowed, "I will every day, *Nonno."*

"Bene," he replied softly, his eyes sparkling with tenderness.

He turned to Sir and said under his breath, *"Lui mi manca così tanto…"*

"Sì," Sir answered, his eyes filling with tears.

"We all miss him," Aunt Fortuna choked out, dabbing her eyes again. She then asked Sir, "How is your mother? You should know that I liked her very much when we first met, and we all respect that she is a part of you."

Sir shook his head, muttering, "I can't…" He turned away, looking over the rolling Tuscan hills.

Nonna grabbed Brie's arm and asked beseechingly, "Ruth, Brianna?"

Brie forced a smile, knowing Sir did not want what happened to his mother to taint this moment with his family. "After a difficult season there is finally peace between them."

Aunt Fortuna shared her words with the grandparents, who visibly relaxed upon hearing the news.

Sir glanced at Brie and nodded in gratitude. *"Sì, pace,"* he assured his grandmother, able to look her in the eye when he said it.

"Ti amava," Nonna said simply.

Aunt Fortuna agreed with her. "Yes, your father loved you very much, Thane. You were *the* most important thing to him. More important than the fame or even his beloved violin. I never thought anything could replace his love of that instrument until you came along. I will never forget the look in his eye when Alonzo held you in his arms. He was meant to be a papa—just like you."

Sir seemed deeply moved by his aunt's words, his lips twitching as he tried to rein in his emotions.

It was heartwarming to know that Sir's family had the power to break down the walls he'd so carefully built over the years. They were a source of strength and grounded him in ways no one else could, not even herself.

"*Vi amo tutti*," Sir said, his voice quavering slightly.

"We love you too, Thane," Aunt Fortuna responded and all four embraced in a group hug, Nonna held out her arm, inviting Brie to join them

A pleasant prickling sensation coursed through Brie as she wrapped her arms around Nonna and Aunt Fortuna becoming part of the group. It was the same feeling Brie got whenever something significant happened in her life.

"*Famiglia*," she sighed in contentment.

Before they left the garden, Sir picked the head of a white rose and tucked it behind Brie's ear. "You saved me back there, wife. The wording of your answer about my mother was perfect and allowed me to look Nonna in the eye when I spoke about it."

"It was simply the truth."

He leaned down to sniff the flower and then squeezed her lightly. "I'm fortunate to have partnered with an intelligent woman who also happens to be fast on her feet." He pulled out a white lace ribbon from his pocket.

"You're going to blindfold me again?" she laughed.

"No, téa."

Her body tingled upon hearing her sub name.

He braided her hair and finished it with the ribbon.

She touched the thick braid tentatively, asking, "What's this for, Master?"

"You must wait to find out."

Her heart fluttered. What did Sir have planned for her today—her first full day as his wife?

"We will be taking the train to reach our first destination."

"First?" she asked in surprise.

"I have several stops planned, my dear."

Brie smiled to herself, stroking her braid and silently thanking fate, God, and all the stars above for her incredible luck.

Sir drove her back down the hills of Tuscany, stopping at a switchback so they could spend a moment appreciating the stunning vista. He got out of the car, took a deep breath and sighed. "There is nothing like the sweet air of this place."

Brie took in its sweetness and nodded. "Who knew

air could smell delicious? Maybe it's all the grapes in the area."

Sir chuckled. "Possibly."

"So where are we headed, husband?" she asked when they returned to the car.

"I'm taking you to the floating city."

Her eyes widened in excitement. "We're going to Venice?"

Sir took her hand and kissed it tenderly. "I am going to show you a side of Venezia tourists never see."

Brie felt a shiver of anticipation travel down her spine. The Italian city of canals had always seemed romantic to her, and now she was headed to it on her honeymoon!

Oh, it's good to be Mrs. Thane Davis…

Sir parked his car near the station and grabbed their overnight bag, explaining that the train was the only way onto the island other than by boat. "No cars for the next few days."

Brie liked the idea of that, so not like LA, and she snuggled against him in the seat. An older couple across from them introduced themselves.

The middle-aged woman wearing a sparkly shirt emblazoned with the words "I Love Venice" and a matching hat stuck out her hand. "Hello, my name is Clara Sue and this is my husband Henry. We're from Texas."

Brie took her hand and smiled as she shook it. "It's nice to meet you, Clara Sue and Henry."

"Aren't you the cutest couple?" Clara Sue exclaimed. She elbowed her husband and said, "Wouldn't you agree,

Henry—aren't they an adorable couple?"

He looked at Sir apologetically but dutifully answered his wife, "Yes dear, they are a handsome couple."

"Have you two been to Venice before?" Clara Sue asked.

Sir patted Brie's hand and looked at the woman with a gracious smile. "I have, but this is my wife's first time."

Brie looked up at him adoringly, still mesmerized by the word *wife* being spoken from those gorgeous lips.

"First time, huh?" Clara Sue asked Brie enthusiastically. "Girl, you are in for a treat, let me tell you! Henry and I come here every year—this is going to be our thirty-fifth in Venice. Wouldn't miss it for the world. Would we, honey?"

Henry shook his head. "Never missed a year."

Clara Sue turned her attention back to Sir. "So why has it taken you so long to take her here?"

Sir chuckled lightly. "Actually, we were married yesterday."

Her mouth fell open. "Oh Lord, we have newlyweds." She held up her hand and pointed to them, shouting at everyone on the train, "Newlyweds here! Just married yesterday."

The train broke out in applause as Brie buried her head in Sir's chest.

"So, I take it you're going on a gondola ride first thing. Am I right?" Clara Sue punched her husband in the arm. "I'm right, aren't I?"

Sir raised an eyebrow. "Actually, I plan to whisk my wife off to a hotel room." He produced a length of silky white fabric from his pocket, adding, "A gag, in case she gets a little too enthusiastic for the other guests."

Clara Sue blushed a deep red, her lips making the perfect circular 'o'. She remained like that for several seconds as if frozen in time.

Henry looked at Sir and grinned. "Now that's a first. Never saw my wife speechless before."

Brie held out her left hand to Sir and looked up at him with an innocent expression. "Would you tie it around my wrist for safekeeping, husband?" Sir did as she asked and she brought the soft material to her lips, kissing it lightly. "I can't wait."

Clara Sue said nothing, turning to stare hard out the train window, but Brie didn't miss the quick glances she gave them from time to time the rest of their short trip.

"Enjoy yourselves," Henry said with a grin, tipping his baseball cap before guiding his still blushing wife off the train.

"Nice couple," Sir commented dryly.

Brie giggled. "You have such a subdued but wicked sense of humor, Sir."

He kissed her hand. "It's all you, Mrs. Davis."

As Sir was helping her off the train, several passengers stopped for a moment to congratulate them. It was humbling to have so many take time to wish them happiness, and Brie considered it a good omen for the years ahead.

Sir led her through the train station and out the doors to the famous canals where boats were waiting for passengers.

"This is so exciting, Sir!"

Rather than taking a boat, Sir guided her over a

bridge to the cobbled streets of Venice. The buildings of the city towered above her, majestic in their age and architecture Brie squeaked in delight as she gazed on the numerous shops lined along the streets and the throngs of people gathered from every part of the world.

"So many people," she said breathlessly.

"It *is* a popular place for tourists," he agreed. Sir seemed to know exactly where he was headed, taking her down narrow passageways until he came to a tiny mask shop hidden from the hustle and bustle of the crowded streets.

Brie was intrigued by the mysterious location and eagerly entered the establishment, delighting in the bell that chimed overhead when the door swung open.

A stunning older Italian woman stood up from behind the counter and asked in perfect English, "May I help you, sir?"

Sir smiled at her and answered in Italian. "*Sono venuto per il contatto maschere.*"

Her expression changed into one of recognition. "*Signore* Davis?"

"*Si, signora.*"

The woman's sensual movements were captivating as she gracefully reached up and took two masks from a shelf behind her, wrapping them in delicate tissue paper. She placed them gently into a golden box and tied it with black ribbon.

Brie was surprised that no money was exchanged as the woman bowed to Sir and respectfully handed him the pretty box.

Once out of the shop Brie asked, "How do you

know that woman?"

Sir only smirked, not giving her an answer.

Not one to give up easily, she inquired, "What did you tell her, Sir?"

He looked at Brie in amusement. "I told her I had come for contact masks."

She tilted her head to one side. "What are contact masks, Sir? I've never heard of such a thing."

"Few have, my dear." He nestled the box in one arm and offered his other arm to her.

"And you're not going to tell me?" she said, frowning slightly.

"No, I am not."

Brie stuck out her bottom lip in silent protest.

"Why would I tell you when I can show you?"

Her pout disappeared as a smile crept across her face. "That would be preferable."

Sir shook his head and tsked teasingly. "Your lack of patience is concerning, téa."

Her heart sped up upon hearing her sub name. It meant that the surprise he had planned would be as Master and submissive. How incredibly sexy was that?

"I know I lack patience, husband," she said apologetically as another couple squeezed by them in the narrow passageway.

"In order for you to grow, as a responsible husband, I should test it more often."

"No, please Sir," she begged. "I don't think my heart could handle any more testing."

He chuckled to himself, smiling warmly at a group of young Asian women who were passing by. They took one look at Sir then immediately looked to the ground, twittering like little birds as they passed him.

"I know firsthand the effect that smile can have on a woman," Brie whispered.

"Are you attempting to charm your way out of the current conversation?"

"No, never, Sir."

"Never indeed…" His low laughter echoed through the narrow alleyway—a beloved sound amplified. "Shall we explore Venezia, wife?"

"Please!"

Much to Brie's surprise Venice was a much bigger city than she imagined, a labyrinth of streets only the experienced could hope to navigate. Sir walked it at a leisurely pace, allowing Brie to visit all the little shops that beckoned to her.

Her favorite items were the extensive array of masks. Although Sir already had two in his possession, she bought several more for herself with his urging. "Can I pick you one out as well, Sir?"

"If you'd like."

She asked him to try on an elaborately decorated mask of yellow with a long nose—the kind used by doctors during the plague. Sir did so reluctantly, his lips a thin line of perseverance.

Brie burst out laughing once he put it on. "I'm sorry, Sir, but you look like a scary version of Big Bird from Sesame Street."

He handed it back to her, unamused by her merriment.

She didn't dare ask him to try on another. She

searched every mask shop they came across until she found the one meant for him. It was a simple, masculine eye-mask of white bordered with gold. Black music notes had been artfully painted across it and on the right side was an outline of a violin accented with tiny jewels.

She held it against her chest, knowing it was perfect. Brie walked out of the shop grinning. "I'm done shopping."

"So soon?" he asked, seeming genuinely surprised.

"Yep, I found exactly what I was looking for."

"Although you may be done for today, babygirl, I suspect you will change your mind tomorrow when I take you to the *Ponte di Rialto*."

"Oh…I like the sound of that!"

"I'm certain you'll like it even more when you see what they sell there."

Brie suddenly had images of numerous kinky shops, but not with the normal selection of cheap plastic or rubber versions of sex toys. She figured they must be like the masks, artfully created masterpieces that looked as pleasing to the eye as they were pleasuring for the body. "I can't wait, Sir!"

"Do you know where we are right now?"

She smiled, shaking her head.

"Our honeymoon suite." To Brie's surprise, Sir turned toward the entrance of a regal hotel only a few steps away. One of the waiting doormen swiftly opened the huge glass door, bowing to them as they entered.

The hotel Sir had picked was extravagant in its ornate decorations and majestic foyer. "Oh Sir, this is breathtaking."

He raised an eyebrow, responding in a low voice, "I do plan to take your breath away…shortly."

She felt heat rise to her cheeks as the porter took the overnight bag from Sir, and Brie's armful of packages. Much to her surprise, rather than an elevator, the young man led them up a long flight of stairs and then through a maze of hallways. It was so confusing that Brie doubted she could find her way back out.

The porter explained as they walked, "Our hotel is a very old structure that has been added to over the years. It is the reason for the unique passageways."

"Ah…" Brie appreciated the explanation, noting where the original structure ended and the additions began. Whoever designed it had taken great care to keep the hotel's interior consistent throughout.

She was greatly relieved when the young man finally stopped at a white door decorated with gold vines accented with clusters of grapes. "Your room, Mr. and Mrs. Davis."

"Isn't it beautiful, Sir?" Brie said, tracing the outline of one of the painted gold vines on the wooden door as she stepped inside.

"It's not just beautiful, wife. This room is known for blessing couples with fertility, hence the grapes at the entrance."

Her eyes widened as she looked around the magnificent room, a colorful Venetian sky painted on the ceiling with light fluffy clouds that looked so real she swore they were moving. The oversized wrought-iron bed with its intricate headboard and crisp white linens invited her to lie down and enjoy its comforts, while Venetian glass placed tastefully throughout the room not only added color but spoke of the city's long history. A large bay window overlooking the tiled roofs of Venice added to the overall charm.

Once the porter left, Brie fell onto the bed and declared, "I could stay here forever."

Sir put down the box he carried and moved up to her, loosening the buttons of his collar before rolling up the sleeves of his shirt. Her heart quickened seeing him do that—those simple, telling movements signified he was getting ready to play.

"I want you to strip, téa."

Brie smiled as she got off the bed gracefully.

She gave him a playfully innocent look as she undressed before him, swaying her hips and biting her lip seductively as she removed each piece of clothing.

"That was nice. Now stand on the ledge of the window, facing the city."

Brie gasped, nervous but also exhilarated at the prospect of being on public display. Sir helped her step up to stand on the ledge of the bay window. Completely naked, she looked down at the bustling street below with numerous boats floating past in the canal.

"Spread your legs shoulder-width apart."

She placed each foot in line with her shoulders, exposing herself further to anyone who might happen to look up.

Sir rifled through the overnight bag and produced four pieces of rope. She moaned when she saw them.

His confident smirk was melt-worthy. "That's right, téa, I'm going to tie you up. Displaying you for my pleasure."

Her pussy ached at his pronouncement, her skin tingling when he grasped her left ankle and began binding it. Sir was slow and methodical as he secured each limb, tightening the rope so that she could not move from the position.

Brie continued to watch the people below, her pussy now dripping with excitement.

Sir stood on the ledge behind her and undid the white satin on her wrist. "Open," he growled into her ear. She parted her lips and he placed the material between her teeth, tying it tightly.

What was the reason for the gag? Brie wondered. *What did Sir have planned for her?*

He tilted her head to one side and lightly kissed her as he moved her braided hair to the front, leaving her back unobstructed before stepping back down to admire her.

"My beautiful bride, all tied up, exposed and helpless. Quite an arousing sight."

Brie heard Sir pop a bottle of champagne left by the hotel staff in celebration of their new marriage. She heard him pour a glass for himself before sitting down behind her.

"How does it feel, knowing that at any moment someone might chance to look up to see you naked and bound?"

She groaned into the gag, reminded of the time Rytsar had done something similar to her at his beach house in California. She'd enjoyed the exhibitionism, but the police had been called to check on her that session which made Brie nervous now.

Brie desperately hoped that would not be the case in Venice.

Sir was in no hurry, taking his time sipping the glass of champagne. After he finished, Sir purposely moved their overnight bag from her line of sight before unzipping it to remove something from it.

"Curious, téa?"

She nodded her head vigorously.

"I requested that Marquis make me something for the honeymoon."

Brie moaned in pleasure, knowing he must be holding a flogger in his hand.

"I've been practicing with it for weeks now."

Brie trembled in expectation.

"Are you ready to fly, babygirl?"

She took a deep breath, already feeling the effects of endorphins flowing through her system caused by the simple binding and public display. She closed her eyes, relaxing her muscles as she waited for the beloved stroke of the flogger.

"Keep your eyes open and focused on the people below until I tell you to do otherwise."

Brie opened her eyes and looked down, smiling inside. He knew her so well—knew that she would have missed the full beauty of the scene he'd so thoughtfully created as a gift to her. He was forcing her to be aware and in the moment, not allowing her to fly so quickly she would miss it.

Before Sir began, he turned on a recording of his father's music, letting the lone violin start her on the journey.

Brie let out a long, drawn-out moan when the flogger connected with her skin. The heavy thud of the instrument resonated through her entire body.

She was familiar with its touch… It was a replica of the eighty-tailed flogger Marquis had used when they filmed together. She remembered well the all-encompassing sensation and the two-handed stance the instrument required of the yielder. It made sense now why Sir had needed to practice before using the tool.

Brie's pussy became wetter with each stroke. She could just imagine the way Sir looked as he wielded the mighty instrument and gracefully swung it in the air.

Her eyes rolled back for a moment, the lure of sub-space whispering to her. She resisted its call, forcing herself to look across the canal.

A prick of fear coursed down her spine when she saw a man leaning against an iron lamp post, watching her as he casually dragged on a cigarette.

Brie mumbled in her gag, trying to warn Sir.

He only sounded amused when he asked, "What was that again?"

She shook her head, making an "uh, uh uh" sound indicating 'red'—her preferred safeword.

Sir stopped mid-stroke and came up from behind. "You want me to stop, téa?"

Brie shook her head, but then lifted her chin in the direction of the observer. Sir followed her gaze and then proceeded to chuckle. "I see we have a watcher." He turned his attention back on Brie. "You know it's to be expected when a beautiful woman displays herself in a window. Enjoy the attention."

Before walking away Sir asked, "Do I have permission to continue?"

Even though the watcher made her slightly uneasy, his presence did add an element of the unknown to an already spectacular scene. Because Sir appeared unconcerned, she nodded her consent without further hesitation.

"Good, because I'm about to let you fly."

Brie swayed in her bonds, the promise of flight making her body weak.

"Keep your eyes on your audience until you're unable to focus."

Brie looked down at the stranger as Sir ramped up the strength and speed of his lashings—perfectly timed so that she could anticipate each one, using the volley of continuous strokes to advance herself ever closer to blessed flight.

Her body shook with each contact, and she wondered what the man below could possibly be thinking. Unlike Faelan, who immediately called the authorities when he saw Brie bound and gagged, this man did not seem concerned. Was it possible he knew exactly what was going on, that he might be a part of the BDSM lifestyle himself?

It didn't matter.

Brie was far too close to subspace to prevent what was about to happen. With Sir's permission already given she willingly dived into the sweet abyss. Although she remained partially aware of her surroundings, they became mixed with the delicious feeling the flogger evoked until all became one—all thought stopped as sensation took over.

"Téa… Téa, focus on my voice. It's time to come back to me."

Brie smiled as she slowly blinked her eyes open with great effort. She looked up at her beloved Master and said gruffly, "I'm back."

His lips curled into a pleasant smile. "That was deeper than I expected."

"Must have been the skill of the man behind the instrument."

She realized she was lying on the bed, and turned her head to look at the window where she'd been tied up. "Is the watcher still there?"

"No. I took you down almost an hour ago."

"It's been that long?"

"It has, babygirl. I guess you were well overdue for a long flight."

She purred. "It was heaven, Sir."

"Although I am glad, I have more planned for us tonight. Now I'm doubting if you can handle it."

She attempted to sit up in the bed to prove she was ready and able to handle anything he had planned. However, her muscles were slow to respond despite her eagerness, not fooling Sir in the least.

"Maybe a little food would perk me up?" she suggested, not wanting to miss out on the evening's festivities.

"A nutritious indulgence is in order," he agreed.

Sir picked up the hotel phone, speaking to the desk clerk in Italian. Afterwards, he got off the bed and walked over to their bag, tossing something to her nonchalantly.

"Better get dressed before the hotel staff arrives. No undergarments permitted."

Brie grinned as she stood up feeling more alert already, excitement coursing through her at the promise of further play. She made her way to the bathroom and squealed in delight when she saw the antique claw-foot tub.

"I love it!" she cried through the open door. "This place is pure perfection."

Sir said nothing, so Brie hurried to freshen up before slipping on the dress he'd given her. It wasn't until the light material slid down her body that Brie realized it was a new dress—another gift from him.

Brie stared in the mirror in awe. The dress was white chiffon, a simple cut with a flared skirt. It was modest in style, but the innocence of it was deceptively sexy, especially since she was wearing nothing underneath.

Her nipples protruded flirtatiously under the thin material, making her feel and look deliciously naughty. Brie untied the white lace in her hair used to secure her braid, and fluffed out her long curls.

She used the length of lace as a headband to hold back the hair from her face and fashioned the ends into a pretty bow. Now she looked the absolute picture of innocence.

Brie walked back out of the bathroom and said shyly, "Master?"

He looked up and warmed the room with his smile. "Yes, my goddess?"

"Thank you for my beautiful new dress."

Sir held out his arms and she glided into them. "You look absolutely fuckable in that dress, téa."

Brie blushed at his praise.

He was leaning down to plant a kiss on her lips when there was a knock on the door.

"Excuse me." Sir walked to the door and opened it to the server. The young man came in asking Sir where he wanted the tray, but when he saw Brie, the server momentarily halted. He starred at her for several moments before regaining his senses and placing the tray on the table. He quickly retreated to the door, closing it behind him without waiting for his tip.

"It appears I am not the only one who thinks you're fuckable."

Brie giggled. "Must be this room and all the fertility blessings floating about…" She looked down at her pretty dress again and twisted from side to side. "Or maybe this dress had something to do with it."

Sir pulled her to him, growling, "No to all of the above. It has everything to do with the woman *inside* the dress."

He kissed her with such passion that Brie felt butterflies. Instead of throwing her on the bed and taking her, Sir leaned over and lifted the silver lid on the tray, revealing a bowl of fresh strawberries.

"I remember how much you enjoyed these during our bet, téa."

She smirked. "You do realize I'm not in need of an aphrodisiac." Then she added in a more seductive voice, "You see, Master, I'm already quite desperate for your…" She kissed him on the lips before continuing. "Hard…" Moving slowly to his ear, she finally whispered, "Cock."

Sir pressed his hand against his growing erection, shaking his head. "The idea is to build on that feeling—to increase our libido." He took one of the pieces of fruit and held it to her mouth. "For your health and escalating sexual appetite."

"Cruel Master…" she complained, opening her lips to him.

"Take your medicine like a good girl," he murmured when she bit into the succulent fruit. As Brie chewed, he nuzzled her ear before nipping it teasingly. "Even now I long to fill you up until you scream for mercy."

She groaned, her pussy aching for him. "No more, Sir. I *need* you."

He picked up another strawberry. "Yes, more. Take everything I give you tonight, for I promise a thorough fucking at the end." He leaned down and whispered hoarsely, "Like nothing you've experienced, téa."

Brie moaned as she closed her eyes. Despite the electrical hum of desperation and desire she felt for him, she answered dutifully, "If it pleases you, Master."

"It does please me," he replied with a wicked grin. "Finish the strawberries while I get dressed. We have a formal event we've been invited to and I don't want to be late."

Brie watched as Sir undressed. His body still mesmerized her—the dark hair on his chest, the toned muscles of his stomach, those strong protective arms and his masculine thighs…

She had to stop looking or she was afraid she might possibly implode.

Brie got up, searching through the overnight bag for her makeup, but when Sir realized what she was doing, he stopped her. "No, keep your face just as it is. You have no need to improve on perfection."

"Aww…that so sweet of you to say."

"I mean it. There is nothing that could add to your beauty."

She put her hands to her heart in adoration of his praise.

"Except, of course, my cock inside your pussy."

Knowing that wasn't going to happen anytime soon, she murmured, "Evil—you are pure evil, Master."

Sir laughed as he adjusted his tie and buttoned up his jacket.

"So, Sir, if this is a formal gathering, may I ask why I'm naked underneath my dress?"

Sir's eyes sparkled mischievously. "Why indeed?"

Brie fed Sir the last remaining strawberry, wanting to return the favor, but ended up teasing herself in the process as she watched Sir open his lips and lick it before he consumed the red fruit.

Evil to the core…

Before they left the room, Sir instructed her to bring the golden box and answered her question before she even had a chance to ask.

"It's required for entrance, my dear."

The Masquerade

As Sir guided her through the busy streets of Venice, he explained in hushed tones, "The most romantic city in the world also happens to be one of the kinkiest."

Brie's eyes widened as she looked around in surprise. "Really?"

He nodded. "Tonight we will be visiting one of the many underground clubs that only Italians are invited to."

She giggled nervously. "But I'm not Italian, Sir."

"Ah, but you're married to one, Mrs. Davis," her husband answered with a wink.

Brie walked beside Sir with a sense of curiosity as she took extra note of the locals working in the shops and restaurants around her. She'd never known that Venetians were such a kinky people. It made the place feel more like home to her.

She squeezed Sir's hand, "I think I love Venice even more now."

Sir took her through a maze of streets and passageways until they came to a row of what looked to be apartments. There was one door painted a vibrant green. He knocked on it three times, paused and knocked twice more.

After several moments, the door opened. A young woman smiled warmly when she saw the golden package Brie was holding. The lady took it from her and invited them both inside. "*Buonasera.*"

"The woman wished us a good evening, téa. Tell her '*salve*'. It's a formal hello."

Brie bowed slightly and repeated the word, trying to match Sir's Italian accent.

The woman's eyes twinkled as she opened the box and handed them each one of the masks. Brie was stunned by the elegant white mask she was given. It shone with a thousand diamond-like stones, placed carefully to create intricate patterns of ivy. The cut of the openings for the eyes was sensually feminine, with tiny dark stones set around the upper eye openings to mimic long eyelashes.

"Let me tie it for you, téa." Sir offered.

She lifted the mask to her face and felt a sexual surge when he inadvertently touched her while tying it on.

"Turn around and let me look at you," he commanded.

Brie turned to face him and was humbled by the look of admiration she saw in his eyes.

"You, my dear, make the perfect virgin princess."

Brie blushed and urged Sir to don his. She was slightly disappointed that his mask was a simple design—a basic black eye mask with no jeweled accents and nothing to set it apart. However, she had to admit that the color of the mask did complement his handsome face with his dark Italian hair and the sexy five-o'clock shadow covering his jaw. It gave him an air of mystery she found quite alluring.

The woman retied the empty box and placed it on a table that was already full of them. Brie was shocked, wondering how many Italians were attending this private event.

Their hostess smiled graciously as she ushered them up the stairs.

"How formal is this event, Master?" Brie asked nervously as she climbed the many steps.

"There is no reason to worry, téa. There are no sadists or traditionalists at this gathering, only people who wish to connect on a deeper level."

It was a great relief to Brie knowing she wouldn't have to worry about strict protocol. It was distracting to constantly concern oneself about inadvertently looking a Dom in the eye or failing to keep the proper distance behind one's Master.

When they reached the top step, the area opened up to reveal a room full of exquisitely dressed people, all wearing elaborate masks that kept their faces hidden.

The room itself was covered in plush purples and rich golds, from the couches, wall coverings and drapes, to the paintings on the ceilings. All of it gave off an aura of intrigue and elegance. It felt to Brie as if she'd stepped back in the time to the days of lords and ladies of old.

Their hostess announced them to the gathering. "*Presentando il figlio del Maestro Alonzo Davis e la sua nuova sposa Brianna.*"

The assembly clapped as one of the men broke off from a small group and walked over to speak with them. He held out his hand to Sir. "It is an honor to have you and your new bride join us tonight, Sir Davis."

"The honor is mine, *Signore Savino*."

Brie was surprised to hear the man speak English when all she heard around her was Italian. Remembering her manners, she bowed her head and said, "*Grazie, Signore Savino*."

He eyed her appreciatively. "You are a pretty little thing. I can see why Sir Davis was so quick to claim you."

"Téa is like my father in spirit. A positive force."

It was the first time Sir had ever compared her to his father. Brie was deeply moved, but could only respond with a squeeze of her hand.

"Then you are fortunate, Sir Davis. A beauty in body and soul."

"I quite agree. Don't let us disturb your prior conversation. Please return to your guests," Sir stated.

Signore Savino nodded amiably. "Everyone knows who you are, so feel free to join any group. We are all pleased you have joined us tonight." The distinguished gentleman turned to Brie and took her hand to kiss it. "I hope you enjoy your evening, Mrs. Davis. I know Dante is looking forward to connecting with you."

Brie smiling politely, but shot a surprised look in Sir's direction when the man turned away.

Sir's confident expression eased her misgivings. She knew he had planned this night around her so there was no reason to worry—only to anticipate.

He led Brie to a group of three on the other side of the room. She did not miss the lustful glances in her direction as they passed through the crowd. Her nipples contracted in response to the attention, garnering second and third glances.

Having Sir by her side meant she could thoroughly enjoy the silent admiration of the other guests. It was what Sir desired, so she held her head high but at a respectful angle, confident in the knowledge she was his and his alone.

Being a strictly Italian event, it made sense to Brie that Italian was spoken. However, it left her oblivious to the many conversations, although she did smile and nod whenever people laughed, wanting to feel a part of the group.

It was at that moment Brie decided it was her duty to learn the language. With a husband of Italian descent who was proud of his heritage, it only made sense she should become fluent in it.

She looked to the floor, smiling to herself, having determined to do it in secret so she could surprise Sir. The thought of the expression on his face when she answered him with perfect clarity and pronunciation made her giddy with joy.

Sir interrupted her thoughts by asking, "This young man just asked what has you smiling so. I must admit that I'm curious as well."

Brie looked up to see a young man with wavy brown hair and dark brown eyes standing to the left of her. She noted he was wearing a mask similar to hers in color and shape.

She answered Sir, not wanting to lie to him but also hoping not to spoil her future surprise, "I was just thinking what a lovely language Italian is. It sounds so beautiful, like music rolling off the tongue."

Sir repeated her words to the man. He nodded to her in answer, a slight smile on his lips. He said something back to Sir and waited for him to translate.

"He would agree," Sir said, "but adds that the Italian language is not just about the words spoken. It's about the expression of the hands." Brie didn't miss the glint in Sir's eyes as he repeated the young man's reply.

Her curiosity was piqued, wondering at the meaning behind his words. She turned to the handsome Italian, bowing her head slightly. "*Sì.*"

Another group gestured to Sir, wanting to speak with him. The two made their way over to the large group where she heard Alonzo's name mentioned several times. Since Brie could not keep up with the conversation, she stood quietly beside Sir taking the opportunity to glance around the room. She felt a chill when she suddenly realized that everyone in attendance seemed to have a mask paired with someone else—everyone except Sir.

She looked up at him questioningly during a lull in the conversation and asked, "Is there a reason you and I are not wearing matching masks?"

"I wondered when you would notice, téa."

"What is the significance, Master?"

"Everyone will partner up according to their corresponding masks."

"But what about you?"

"I get to sit back and watch."

"And me?"

"As I'm sure you have already surmised, you'll be partnering with the young man who just spoke to you."

Brie's heart began to race knowing that Sir was asking her to scene tonight with a complete stranger. "What I am expected to do, Master?"

"This is a unique group, my dear. Their emphasis is on communicating sensuality through touch only. You know I have always maintained that touch is the most effective tool in the BDSM arsenal."

"Yes, Master. You have taught me that time and time again."

"Well, tonight I want you to enjoy the touch of a stranger, but there will be no intercourse involved." He placed his hands on her stomach possessively. "I protect what's mine."

Brie put her hand on top of his, smiling apprehensively.

"I can see the hesitancy in your eyes, téa, but I take pleasure in seeing you challenged."

Brie glanced at the young man who was now gazing directly at her with unveiled interest.

"Are you willing?" Sir asked.

She felt the butterflies start as she looked up at her Master, answering in the barest of whispers, "Yes."

Sir nodded to the young man across the room, who proceeded to excuse himself from the group he was talking with and walked over to join Sir and Brie.

"Téa, this is Dante."

Brie smiled shyly as Sir continued. So this was Dante, the one Signore Savino had mentioned earlier.

Sir introduced Brie formally to the young man in his native tongue.

Under her breath Brie asked, "Does he speak English, Master?"

"Why don't you ask him yourself, little sub?"

Brie was unsure how to ask her question in Italian, so she kept it simple, *"Inglese?"*

Dante shook his head with a charming grin.

She sighed to herself, finding the lack of verbal communication both intimidating—and a little sexy.

Sir tilted her chin up, declaring with a smirk, "I don't think verbal skills will be an issue tonight."

Brie had experienced a similar dynamic with Rytsar on their first meeting. It added an element of mystery, but also made the power exchange that much more challenging.

Touch is a universal language, Brie reminded herself.

Dante pointed to the bar, indicating that he wanted to get her a drink. She requested the only drink she knew how to say in Italian. *"Vino, per favore."*

"Rosso o bianco?"

She smiled, knowing he was asking if she wanted red or white. Since red wine seemed to have an amorous effect on her, she answered, *"Rosso, grazie signore."*

Brie wanted to pat herself on the back when Dante nodded his head and walked off to fulfill her wishes without any further questions.

Sir chuckled under his breath. "Starting to feel a little more Italian, are we, téa?"

She blushed. "I have such a long way to go. But yes, Master, I'm beginning to feel as if I belong here."

"*Bene*," he said, bending down and growling seductively in her ear. "But never forget your own heritage. It makes you who are you."

Gratitude coursed through her. Sir wasn't asking her to change, only to meld the richness of his culture and people into her own life experiences. Again, Brie was struck by how blessed she was to have coupled with such a man.

Dante impressed Brie when he returned with a glass of wine not only for her, but for Sir as well. He then left her with a respectful bow.

"Gracious, isn't he, Master?" she stated as he walked away.

"Yes, a man worthy of your attention," Sir replied smoothly, taking a sip from the glass. "Damn," he exclaimed after tasting it, "I do enjoy the flavor of an old vine."

Brie took her own sip. "These must have been happy grapes, because they're partying in my mouth."

Sir laughed out loud, causing some of the other guests to turn and look at them. He simply raised his glass and said, "Uva felici!"

People smiled and raised their glasses in response.

Brie whispered, "What did you say to them?"

"Happy grapes," he answered, winking at her.

She loved that he had a sense of humor. Brie remembered how serious he'd seemed when they'd first met. It wasn't until he'd made a joke about loving the taste of Brie that she came to understand he had a quiet but wicked sense of humor. While Sir wasn't a prankster like Master Anderson or a roguish sadist like Rytsar, he had his own brand of humor which Brie adored.

A beautiful chime sounded from a corner of the room, and as if by magic all the people began moving across the floor like graceful dancers, separating themselves into matching pairs. Dante returned to Brie with an engaging smile playing on his lips.

"It's time, téa," Sir announced as he stepped back from her so Dante could take his place. Brie watched as her Master walked over to a black leather chair and sat down, sipping his wine as he quietly observed her.

Dante put his finger under her chin to direct Brie's eyes back on him.

Her heart skipped a beat knowing she was now under this stranger's control. She knew that she was expected to keep her attention solely on him.

Brie hesitantly looked up at the young Italian, drawn in by those soulful dark brown eyes behind his white mask. She thought by his boyish features he must be younger than her, yet his eyes expressed both depth and wisdom which belied his years. She found him intriguing and wondered about the young Dom's history.

Dante guided her to a sofa covered in red leather and gestured that she should sit. Brie did so slowly with mastered grace, quite aware that Sir was watching her every move. The young Dom took the wine glass from her hand and set it on an end table.

He then undid his tie and laid it across the arm of the sofa. He unbuttoned his shirt next, watching her intently as he slipped it off his shoulders and laid it beside the tie. The young man's chest was bare and less muscular than Sir's, but he sported six-pack abs and a sexy V muscle that was quite attractive.

Dante sat down beside her now bare-chested and tilted his head charmingly as he waited for her to do the same.

She glanced around the room and noticed that all of the guests were similarly undressed—the masculine chests of the men contrasted beautifully with the women's more feminine forms.

With fingers shaking slightly, Brie lowered the straps of her dress one at a time and let the material fall to her waist, exposing her breasts to him. She reminded herself to breathe as he stared down at her chest unashamedly, smiling to himself.

"Bellissimo."

Although being naked before strangers was not new to her, there was something distinctly different about this encounter with Dante. She felt more naked somehow, even though she knew there were only two sets of eyes on her—Sir's and this handsome young stranger's.

Dante's intense stare was disconcerting, causing her to flush all over.

The moans and gasps as the couples around them began exploring each other with their hands and lips only intensified the sexual excitement Brie was experiencing.

Goosebumps rose on her skin when Dante raised his hand to touch one of her breasts. However, his hand stilled before making contact, lingering over it like a promise.

She stared at his masculine hand, feeling like a frightened rabbit, and then looked up into his dark brown eyes wondering what he wanted.

"*Sì?*" he whispered hoarsely.

He was waiting for permission from her. Ever the gentleman…

Brie held her breath when she nodded, her whole body tingling with anticipation as she waited for the first contact.

His touch was incredibly light and hesitant as he caressed her skin. He purposely avoided her hardening nipple. It made her heart beat even faster, the tender way he explored her with his fingers.

Brie had assumed he would be aggressive, passionate and demanding. Instead, Dante's caresses reminded her of a young lover touching the object of his romantic obsession for the very first time.

It was unexpected and unbelievably arousing.

When he finally brushed her aching nipple, Brie surprised herself by crying out as a wave of sensual heat traveled straight to her pussy.

A slight smile curved on Dante's lips at the sound of her pleasure, as the Dom purposely moved his attention to her other breast.

Brie stared at him in wonder, shocked that he was able to create such a high level of desire through simple physical contact. She believed it was the way he did it— this stranger using his hands to convey his curiosity about her and his sexual interest.

Dante lightly grazed his palm over her hard nipple, and again she felt the powerful energy transfer to her nether regions, but she was ready for it and did not embarrass herself by crying out this time. Instead, she moaned softly, joining in the chorus of partners around her.

He pulled back from Brie and stared at her for a moment. When she made no move, he took her left wrist and guided her hand onto his pecs. She sucked in her breath as she tentatively caressed the smoothness of his chest, noting the goosebumps starting to rise on his skin from her touch.

The two of them seemed to have a mutual effect on each other.

Unlike Sir, Dante's chest was free of all hair. It felt very different, which made it alluring to her even though she preferred hair. Taking on the role of a young lover, Brie pretended this was her first time seeing a naked man, and gauged her reactions according to the limits of that fantasy.

Her touches were slight and her glances in his direction shy as she touched his hard abs, exploring the lines that separated each muscle. "You are handsome," she murmured.

"*Cosa hai detto?*"

Of course, he couldn't understand her compliment, and she had no clue what he'd just asked. Brie smiled saying the only word she knew that would make sense. "*Bello.*"

He chuckled at her answer, responding, "*Bello? No magnifico o impressionante?*"

She shrugged, giggling self-consciously. Apparently "nice" was not the word he was hoping for.

Dante silenced Brie's giggles by leaning forward to give her a tender kiss. Like his touches, it had the feeling of longing but gentle restraint, as if he were afraid of scaring her away.

Oh Lord, this young Dom knew how to bewitch her. She returned the kiss, pressing her lips against his with equal longing, mixed with the same hesitancy. She pulled away first, briefly smiling at him to let Dante know she'd liked the kiss.

His fingers returned to her, gently caressing her shoulder as he brushed away her hair. Delicious tingles radiated from the point of contact and she purred.

He put his hands on her shoulders and indicated she should turn around. When Brie repositioned her body, she found herself staring straight at Sir from across the room.

Her Master held up his glass to her, encouraging her with his smile as he took a sip of wine. The admiration and pride held in his expression bolstered Brie's courage. Knowing he appreciated the slow progression of the scene emboldened her to continue. She turned her head back toward Dante and tilted her head up, silently requesting a kiss. He leaned over her shoulder and only kissed her cheek.

It made Brie smile. She'd never experienced a Dom like Dante before. He moved her hair forward, covering her breasts with the long brown curls, making a clear path to explore the skin of her back. He ran his hands over her spine so lightly that she involuntarily shivered, causing a new set of goosebumps.

His low chuckle let her know it was the reaction he was hoping for. Although Dante was a complete gentleman, he also appeared to have a mischievous side. The man grazed his fingers under her shoulder blades, running them back up her spine, making her squirm from the insanely light touch.

Then he traced the outline of each rib, purposely challenging her with his ticklish exploration.

Brie cracked, unable to bear the intense tickling, and tried to twist out of his reach. The Dom did not reprimand her. Instead, he wrapped one arm around her waist, pulling her back to him. Dante kissed her neck like a whisper and she moaned from the chills that coursed through her.

Then he started back up with those ticklish caresses, holding her against him when she tried to struggle. She consciously surrendered to the feeling, honoring his dominance by submitting to his will. Once she stilled, those devilish hands then moved back to her breasts, inciting mews of pleasure as he lightly pinched and teased her nipples.

The sexual energy within the room had risen considerably and was now almost a tangible force. She glanced at the couples near her, entranced as she realized each was exploring a different form of sensation play. One was enjoying the relaxing feel of a hair brush as the Dom not only used the instrument for her hair, but to stimulate the skin of her back and arms. Brie was fairly certain the brush would soon be caressing the woman's shapely ass.

A pair of men, one who was completely naked, were exploring the intense stimulation of a Wartenberg wheel. The Dom's skilled hands were spurring a powerful reaction from his partner. The manly groans coming from the submissive male were arousing and Brie felt a gush of wetness between her legs.

She noticed another couple using the delicious caress of a large purple feather. Brie remembered well the feeling and thought back to Faelan and their first scene together. She'd laughed when he'd brought it out, but quickly learned how effective it could be during sensation play.

Brie also recognized a Vampire glove being used on the older woman across the room. It was not a sensation Brie personally cared for but it was clear, based on the woman's expression and vocal responses, that she was savoring its painful caress.

Dante noticed Brie's distraction and responded by lifting her arm above her head. With frightfully slow movements, he ran his fingers over her sensitive armpit. Brie pressed her lips together firmly, keeping still with momentous effort, and was rewarded with a light kiss on her shoulder when he was done. He'd effectively returned her focus back on him with that simple act.

"*Bene…*" the young Dom growled in her ear. He reached back and grabbed something from the end table. Brie was extremely curious what his instrument of sensual pleasure would be. She gazed at Sir and bit her lip before closing her eyes, waiting expectantly for the first touch.

Brie let out a gasp of surprise when heat caressed the nape of her neck. The temperature of it reminded her of candles, but this tool was solid and very smooth. Dante used the thin instrument like an extension of his hand, caressing her skin tenderly with its warmth.

Curiosity got the best of her and she opened her eyes

when Dante brought the tool to her front. She shivered in delight as she watched a thin silver wand glide against her breast, lingering and teasing her nipple.

Brie looked back at Dante and sighed in pleasure. He took the opportunity to kiss her fully on the mouth before returning his attention back onto her nipples. The heat was very conducive to increasing desire and Brie moaned with passion as he traced the roundness of her breasts before heading down to her stomach.

She liked the sexy look of the silver instrument, much like a thin dildo but sleek and elegant. Brie fully expected that Dante would sneak under the material of her dress and help relieve the ache of her pussy, but the wand moved upwards instead. He tilted her head sideways and caressed her neck and the outline of her jaw with the instrument. Another moan escaped her lips as a cascade of shivers took over, causing a small tear of pleasure to run down her cheek. His ability to completely enrapture her with his simple caresses had her spellbound.

Dante kissed away the tear, and then glided the wand over her sensitive lips with the barest of touches. She shivered from the light contact and ran her tongue over her tingling lips. He chuckled softly, following up the wand with his own firm lips.

Brie leaned against him when his tongue entered her mouth and she tasted him for the first time. He flicked his tongue lightly, causing waves of pleasure that traveled downward, making her clit pulse with need.

Dante pulled away and turned Brie back to face him. He stared at her for several moments, drawing her in with his gaze before placing her hand on his chest and leaning in for another kiss. Just before their lips met he stopped, and she instinctively leaned farther to kiss him. He groaned passionately when her lips pressed against his.

Brie joined his vocalizations with moans of her own when he wrapped her in his arms. Her body was burning with sexual energy. It didn't help when she glanced around, noticing that most of the couples were now completely naked and either engaging in oral sex or experimenting with the tools in more intimate ways. However, not *one* couple was having intercourse.

Brie finally understood that the sole focus of this private gathering was centered around connecting through touch, and she found the idea of that extremely alluring. To have a random partner each time and have the opportunity to explore new sensations together would be incredibly sexy.

However, she felt as if she would combust if something wasn't done soon.

She felt the electric jolt of Sir's touch and looked up to see him standing over her. He spoke to Dante briefly in Italian. The young Dom nodded, giving Brie one last kiss on the cheek before exchanging places with Sir and taking his seat at the large chair across from them.

"Téa, stand for me," Sir commanded in a gruff voice.

Brie stood and faced him, her whole body trembling with pent-up desire.

Sir grazed his hand over her bare shoulder, trailing his fingers down her arm. "I was entertained watching the interaction between you two." He leaned down and growled in her ear. "When I say entertained, I mean incredibly turned on."

She looked down and saw the outline of his cock under the dark material of his pants. It was extremely gratifying.

"Watching you reminded me of our nights when you would pose for me. Hours of erotic enjoyment…" He took her in his arms and kissed her hard, releasing the torrent of built-up tension observing her had caused.

Whereas Dante had been gentle and hesitant, Sir was demanding and rough with his kiss, bruising her lips as he plundered her mouth with his tongue.

She moaned in excitement, responding to his need, longing to release her own pent-up desire. When he pulled at her dress, she wondered if he would take her on the couch right then and there, forsaking the rules of the gathering.

Brie desperately hoped so!

She was greedy for his cock and would do anything to feel it inside her. After those many months of forced abstinence, she was insatiable for the man and doubted she would ever get enough of him.

Sir let her dress fall to the floor. Brie stepped out of it and was rewarded with another passionate kiss as he pushed her with his body onto the couch, crushed in his embrace.

It was a natural response for Brie to spread her legs to him, but Sir refused to take advantage of her open invitation. Instead, he stood back up and removed his jacket, shirt and tie. Brie openly admired his handsome form, licking her lips in anticipation and lust.

Sir unbuckled his belt next, slowly pulling it through the loops and laying it beside Brie to tantalize her further before sitting back down next to her. Sir grasped the back of her neck, kissing her hungrily, drinking in the scent of her as he devoured her with his touch.

"Please…" she begged.

Sir put his hand on her throat, pressing firmly. His lips pressed against hers as he thrust his tongue into her mouth. The hold was so dominant and the kiss so possessive after a night of teasing that she orgasmed.

He broke the kiss, releasing his hold on her. "Did you just come, téa?"

"Yes, Master," she panted.

Rather than becoming upset, her answer actually seemed to please Sir. He went back to kissing her again, his hand returning to her throat. His voice was hoarse with desire when he murmured, "Do not give in again until you have my expressed permission."

Brie moaned her agreement as he carried her away with his passion. She fought off the overwhelming need to connect physically as one, although it seemed every cell in her body screamed for it.

Her pussy lifted of its own accord, seeking his attention. Sir's breath became raspy as he got drawn up in the sexual heat between them, almost beast-like in his blind lust for her. He placed his hand on her mound and then froze.

Without explanation, Sir pulled away.

"Don't stop," she whimpered.

Sir took a deep breath, shaking his head several times to regain focus. He stood up and picked up her dress, motioning to Dante. The young Dom came over and took the dress. Sir ordered gruffly, "*Vestire la ragazza.*"

Without hesitation, Dante lifted the dress over Brie's head and let it fall around her, then he turned Brie around to face Sir.

Brie looked at her Master questioningly, wondering if she had done something wrong.

Sir read the concern on her face and confided in a low voice, "The control I wish to have versus the control I actually have right now demands you cover up before I break house rules."

He gave orders to Dante in Italian, then asked Brie to lay on the lounger face down, her chin resting on the unused armrest with her ass presented to him. She followed his instructions, anxiously waiting for his next command.

She heard the clank of the belt when he picked it up from behind her and readied herself. Instead of smacking her ass with it, Sir looped it around her neck, making her groan in both surprise and pleasure.

Dante surprised Brie further by getting down on his knees beside her. Sir pulled on the belt, providing enough pressure to state his dominance. In that deliciously raw submissive pose, Dante gave her the barest of kisses as Sir's hands glided over the back of her thighs.

Her pussy contracted with desire. The kiss of the stranger along with the electric touch of her Master sent her near the precipice.

"The smell of your excitement is driving me insane, babygirl," Sir growled lustfully. "I've never been so close to the edge in public, not even that night at the opera when all I wanted to do was pull you to me and fuck you hard."

"Oh, Master…" she panted in desperation, recalling that night when he had played out her fantasy as her Khan. It only made her need him more.

"We have to make an early exit. I know my limits." Sir leaned down and whispered in her ear, "However, I want you to come just once more. I take great pleasure in feeling you orgasm against my tongue."

Brie moaned as he positioned himself behind her and opened her legs wider. At Sir's signal, Dante moved in for another kiss while Sir's tongue made contact with her swollen clit.

Just a couple of flicks from his skilled tongue and Sir had her riding the wave of an intense orgasm. She kissed Dante deeply as her pussy pulsed against Sir's mouth, the pressure of the belt around her neck helping to increase the power of her climax.

Dante groaned, becoming an integral part of the connection between Sir and Brie. When Sir pulled away, he said to her in admiration, "You're primed like I have never seen before, téa. Two orgasms with the minimum of external stimulation."

She turned her head back toward him. "I think if your cock were to touch my pussy right now I would gush with another come."

Sir backed away from her as if she were fire, his hard cock straining against his pants. "I believe we are done here."

Sir grabbed his shirt, buttoning it up quickly while

speaking to Dante. The young Dom nodded his under-standing and turned to Brie, taking her hand to kiss it—the feel of his lips lingering on her skin.

"*Ciao, bella.*"

"Ciao," she replied, but Brie stood on tip-toes and kissed him on the cheek, adding, "*Grazie mille,*"—thank you a thousand times.

The smile that spread across his face was enchanting. Dante shook Sir's hand next, giving him a respectful handshake.

Sir pulled him in closer, patting him on the back. It was the handshake Sir only used with close friends, and it made Brie wonder exactly who Dante was and if there was history between him and Sir.

Before she could ask, she found herself whisked out of the room by her Master. He made a beeline through the multitude of couples still enjoying themselves. On their way out, Sir paused for a moment to take off the mask and lay it on the table next to the golden boxes. Brie did the same, sad that she had to give up her beautiful mask. She lay it next to Sir's, struck by the perfect contrast of the black mask beside the white.

She grazed her fingers over both lovingly, smiling to herself as they left.

Romance in Venezia

Sir took in the night air once they stepped outside. There were a number of ominous clouds advancing on the city, their massiveness highlighted by occasional flashes of lightning as the sound of far-off thunder echoed in the distance. The air was tinged with the scent of the oncoming storm.

After several deep breaths of fresh air, he stated, "Fuck, that was close."

Brie smiled up at him, thrilled that the scene he'd created had almost gotten the best of him. Although it didn't relieve the raging ache in her own loins, at least she knew he was as desperate for her as she was for him.

However, she couldn't fathom why he was torturing them both. "So we're headed back to the hotel then?"

He shook his head, his expression serious. "No, babygirl, the night's just begun for us."

"What about the storm?"

"It will only add to the experience," he assured her. The glint in his eye spurred her to take hold of the arm he offered. She was convinced that their mutual relief was close at hand.

Sir led her through the dark streets of Venice. It looked completely different in the evening. The numerous shops, constant chatter and bright colors were gone—replaced with empty streets and quiet alleyways.

She snuggled up against to him as they walked, appreciating this shared experience. Although she had a million questions about Dante and the club they'd just visited, she kept them to herself. There was something special about this moment, and she didn't want to disturb it with questions that could wait.

The two walked in silence together, both keenly aware of the other. The night ahead might be a challenging lesson in patience for Brie—for Sir as well—but that made it all the more alluring.

Sir seemed to know exactly where he was going, guiding Brie through the maze of streets until they reached a large piazza next to an impressive cathedral. Her jaw dropped when she saw that the entire courtyard was covered in seawater. "What's happened here?"

"Several times a year the sea covers the Piazza San Marco at night."

She shook her head, amazed and a little frightened by it, wondering if all of Venice might someday be swallowed up by the sea surrounding it.

Holding out his hand, Sir asked, "Care to have a little fun, téa?"

Brie glanced around, noting a few tourists taking pictures as they walked around the outskirts of the flooded area, trying their best not to get wet. She wondered what Sir could possibly have in mind, but answered him with a confident smile as she grasped his hand. "Let's."

He twirled her around once and dipped her low, smiling as he said, "We'll need to take our shoes off first."

Her curiosity was piqued as he slipped out of his shoes and stripped off his socks, placing them on the cathedral steps. Not wanting to be left behind, Brie kicked off her heels and placed them next to his shoes.

"You only live once," he said with a charming smile, taking her hand and leading her straight into the water—to the very center of the flooded piazza. Brie giggled in surprise as she followed, watching the water splash around them as they trudged through it.

Once in the middle, Sir took her left hand in his and rested the other on the small of her back. "Shall we dance, wife?"

Brie looked up at him in wonder. "Please, husband."

Sir smiled down at her as he guided her through the water in a slow waltz. The sea water slowed their movements, but added an element of whimsy and elegance as he used the splashing to accent his moves.

He took her breath away when he dipped her again, so low that her hair touched the water. He brought her back up, kissing her deeply before stepping back to twirl her again.

People on the outskirts of the water began taking pictures as Sir carried Brie along in their dance. In her mind, she heard the melody of his father's haunting violin that was played at their wedding, and felt certain by the timing of Sir's moves that he was hearing the same.

Brie looked up at the few remaining stars peeking through the clouds as they danced in the waters of Venice.

The fairy tale is complete…

By the time their impromptu waltz ended the bottom of Brie's dress was soaking wet. Sir guided Brie back to the steps to the applause of the remaining tourists.

"Take a bow, Brie," Sir commanded as he sat down on the steps of St. Mark to put on his socks and shoes.

Brie did as she was told, waving to the people as she took another bow when the applause continued. "I don't think they see that every day," she remarked as she slipped on her heels. "In fact…"

When she didn't finish her thought, Sir asked, "What?"

"I never imagined you would do something like this, Sir."

He shrugged. "It seemed appropriate. An opportunity I would regret not taking advantage of in the years to come."

She hugged him tight. "A night of sensual exploration, and now a romantic dance in the piazza? You continue to enchant me, but I must admit I long to go back to hotel room and experience *you* again."

Sir chuckled softly. "Patience, wife."

Because a young couple was passing nearby, Brie replied demurely, "Let me put it this way. I would be incredibly receptive to any attention a certain part of your anatomy might provide."

He raised an eyebrow and answered with a smirk, "I have every intention of fulfilling that request."

"Thank goodness!"

"But not yet."

Brie groaned.

"I can't have you visit Venezia without experiencing what I have planned next."

The storm was moving in quickly, causing the remaining tourists to hurry along before the dark clouds broke open and baptized the city with fresh rain.

However, Sir seemed in no hurry as the clouds continued to mount. He kept his leisurely pace as they walked beside the canal.

Being unconcerned about the rain since they were already partially wet, Brie strolled beside with him, basking in the fact she was alone with Sir…in Venice.

Much to Brie's delight, Sir led her to where a row of gondolas were docked, but there was only one gondolier still remaining by his vessel—all the others having abandoned their posts because of the advancing storm.

Brie grinned. "A gondola ride, Sir?" It seemed so vanilla and touristy, but still so wonderfully romantic to her.

"It's a must whenever you visit the city for the first time," he stated.

The gondolier wore a silver mask over his eyes and a single spiked leather cuff on his left wrist. Was it possible he was a kinkster like them? Was there such a thing as BDSM gondoliers?

Brie giggled at the thought until the man said, "Welcome, Sir Davis. I am at your command."

"Thank you for waiting, Alberto. I know you must be concerned about the storm."

He looked up and shrugged. "It won't rain for another hour. I know these things. The clouds speak to me." The gondolier smiled at Brie as he held out his hand and helped guide her onto the boat. Once settled, Alberto offered Sir a blanket which he placed over both his lap and hers.

Brie appreciated the warmth and snuggled even closer to Sir.

"Where to, Sir Davis?"

"I leave that up to you, Alberto. You know your city."

The man grinned. "True. I have been here all my life and couldn't imagine ever leaving it." They started out, drifting away from the dock. The boat gently rocked as small waves splashed against it. "It is good that you chose to ride at night, Sir Davis. The daytime is for tourists."

"Agreed. Venezia can only be appreciated for its old-city charm when it is quiet."

"Si."

Brie was entranced as Alberto guided them through the narrow alleyways of water. Above them Venetians were busy having dinner, their windows thrown open and the aroma of their cooking drifting down to the water. She could hear the clink of plates and the hearty conversations and laughter at the tables. Life was happening above them in the little apartments as they floated past in their gondola. It brought Brie immense joy to hear it.

"Lay back," Sir commanded gently.

Brie lay her back against his broad chest and looked

up at the dark sky above. The stars were blotted out by the clouds, but in their stead a beautiful light show was taking place, and the sounds of it rumbled through the city.

"It's like Nature is celebrating with fireworks…" she muttered. "This is incredible, Sir."

"Yes, it is," he agreed, nibbling on her ear. "It inspires me to create my own fireworks."

Brie felt his cold hand slip under her dress to caress her warm sex. She squeaked when he made contact. "So cold!"

She was turned on by the temperature difference and lifted her head toward him, hoping for a kiss.

Sir did not disappoint, his warm lips descending on hers as his chilled fingers moved to more fully explore her bare mound. Brie's nipples hardened at the delicious contrast, and she struggled not to move as one of his fingers slipped inside.

She inadvertently glanced at Alberto and he nodded. The man was fully aware of what was going on underneath the blanket, but she didn't need to be concerned because he was one of them.

Brie closed her eyes for a moment to take in the feel of her Master's finger as his hot breath warmed her cold neck.

"Would you like me to bite you?"

"Please…" she moaned.

Sir bit down, sinking his teeth into the delicate skin of her neck with just enough force to cause that instinctual reaction of surrender she craved.

Her pussy contracted around his finger, letting him know just how much she enjoyed the attention. His low groan was meant only for her, telling Brie how much her desire pleased him.

With slow, unhurried movements he stoked the fire that was already raging inside. Her pussy was primed and ready for him, burning in need for the feel of his hard cock. A night of sensual teasing and romantic interludes had her flying on an emotional and physical high.

"God, I want you..." she panted, pressing against his hand, imploring him to take her.

"In time, babygirl," he answered, pulling his finger from her. Sir *tsked* when she whimpered in protest. "Patience is a skill you need to master, wife, especially if you plan on being a mother."

Hearing him speak of her motherhood had her imagining their tiny child—a physical representation of their love—cradled in her arms. It about did her heart in. "Sir, you play me like a violin."

Sir snorted, kissing the top of her head. "It stands to reason, I suppose. My father was a concert violinist and you, my dear, are very easy to play."

She smiled, charmed again by his sense of humor.

"Now lie back and let your husband caress your breasts while Alberto shares his city with us."

Brie lay back against him and relaxed in his embrace. Sir nonchalantly slipped off the straps from her shoulders, easing the material of her dress down to uncover her breasts. He began slowly trailing his fingers over the round fullness of them, his touch light but not ticklish.

She sighed in contentment as she watched the heavenly light show above her. Had any woman in history experienced what she was experiencing now—lying in the arms of her lover in a gondola as she floated through the city of Venice in the dark under the impressive carpet of electric skies, caressed by his hand while they silently explored the ancient city together?

Brie suspected that even the queens of the past had never known such luxury. "I am truly the luckiest woman on earth," she told Sir, tilting her head back to look at him. "You are my dream come true."

"Since I can also be your worst nightmare, it's good there is a balance."

Brie shook her head, giggling as she settled back against him. "I like your many sides, Thane. It makes you interesting."

"Interesting is a generous word for it."

She opened her mouth to protest.

"Not another word, wife. Relax and savor the experience."

Brie rested against him, squirming occasionally when he tweaked her nipple or bit lightly on her skin.

Pure romantic bliss…

As the dock came into sight, Brie pulled up the straps of her dress while Sir folded the blanket and set it aside. He exited the boat first so he could assist Alberto as they both helped Brie onto the dock.

Sir tried to pay the man but Alberto refused, saying, "Sir Davis, I know who your father is and could never accept monetary compensation from his son. His music changed my life. This was my honor."

"I appreciate your generosity, b—" Sir began, trying again to hand over the bills, but Alberto interrupted him, sounding offended.

"Absolutely not, Sir Davis."

"Very well, then." Sir tucked the money back in his jacket before placing his hand over his heart. "A sincere thank you is in order for such a generous gift."

The man nodded his acknowledgement.

"May I have your business card?"

"Of course, Sir Davis." The gondolier retrieved a card from his breast pocket and handed it to him. "If you are planning on staying, I would like to invite you to my home for lunch. Any day that's convenient for you."

"I'm afraid we will be leaving Venezia tomorrow."

This was news to Brie and she listened more attentively, wondering if he would reveal their next destination.

"I understand, but should you visit my city again the offer still stands." Alberto insisted.

Sir pulled out his business card, handing it over. "Thank you, and I extend the same invitation should you ever find yourself in LA. It would an evening well spent, talking about my father and the influence he had in your life."

"Ciao, Sir Davis." He tipped his hat to Brie. "And Signora Davis."

"Ciao, Alberto," Brie said, honored to have spent the evening with the man.

Sir put his hand on the small of her back as they walked away. "And now just one more stop, babygirl…"

Passion in the Streets

S ir led her along in the same leisurely fashion as they passed the flooded piazza once more. There were no tourists to be seen when the first drops of rain began to fall, dotting the surface of the water in playful patterns as the thunder rolled above them.

"Come, Brie," Sir said, taking her hand. Instead of heading to the hotel, Sir dragged her into a darkened alley, just past the piazza. He pushed her against the marble wall, kissing her roughly. Afterward he growled in her ear, "I've been patient enough. I want you to suck my cock—now."

Brie's heart quickened, realizing he was going to give her what she'd been craving for hours. She immediately sank to her knees, ignoring the hardness of the cobblestone as she unzipped his pants and freed his shaft from his briefs. The heat radiating from his manhood attested to how much Sir needed release.

When she opened her lips wide he cautioned, "Don't take me too deeply in that pink mouth."

Brie's eyes widened at the unusual command. Sir

wasn't normally one to ask her *not* to deep-throat him. Honoring his request, however, she took hold of his shaft and began licking the end of it before putting her lips around the smooth head of his cock.

It was covered in pre-come, alerting her to just how close Sir was to orgasming—and it totally inspired her. Brie was slow and gentle as she teased his shaft, giving it tender kisses while only lightly sucking.

Sir put his hand on her head to prevent her from going deeper, but it was totally unnecessary. She obeyed his command not only because she was devoted to him, but because she wanted that cock deep inside her when he finally came.

Brie grazed his shaft with her teeth, something she knew he enjoyed, but he pulled away from her and ordered huskily, "Stand now."

In the falling rain, Brie stood and faced Sir. He leaned his body weight on her, pressing Brie against the cold marble. Sir's hand disappeared under her dress as his fingers sought out her sex. "I *need* to taste your come," he growled into her ear as he began to pump her with his fingers.

Brie tilted her head up into the cold rain, willing her body to relax. Having ridden the tide between denial and orgasmic release all day, she knew the incredibly intense climax he was seeking from her.

She started to groan loudly as he hit her g-spot with the hard, rapid pace that always invoked a watery come. "Oh God…oh God!" she screamed as a crash of thunder sounded above them, reverberating through the city and her soul.

Brie's body tensed just before it rushed with an earthshattering explosion, momentarily stealing her senses. Sir grunted in satisfaction as he buried his mouth on her mound, licking her freshly-come pussy as he held her in place.

"Fuck, babygirl, you taste so damn good…"

Her legs trembled in the aftermath of the orgasm while Sir continued his attention on her clit. "Please Sir," she panted, "—you."

Sir stood, swiping his mouth as he stared at her with the lust of a hungry wolf. Without warning, Sir grabbed the back of her thighs and lifted her upward, pressing her against the cold wall. Brie squealed in surprise at his strength.

He gripped his rock hard shaft and forced it inside her. Brie let out a cry of passion and relief as he started pumping. She reveled in the fiery ache his cock caused as he stroked her hard.

But Sir needed more and tilted her hips, ramming his cock even deeper. The depth and angle took her breath away and she struggled to take it. Sir dug his fingers into her thighs as he ramped up the tempo.

Brie was both thrilled and frightened by the ferocity of his pounding. He bruised her body as he fucked her without mercy, but all she could cry was, "More… more…"

The rain fell in huge droplets as the lightning lit up the whole sky. Sir lifted his head up and let out a primal roar. Brie gripped onto him in desperation as he gave her the fucking of her life.

The two of them stared at each other in silence after

he came deep inside her, shocked by the intensity of the animalistic coupling. Sir kissed Brie several times before he carefully set her on the ground and helped steady her when she swayed, still weak from the experience.

Brie could only lay against the wall for support as she recovered. "What was that?"

"*That* is how babies are made."

Brie smiled, but it soon disappeared as she felt a powerful urge to fuck him again. She stared at him lustfully, leaning forward for a kiss.

Sir held her back. "Hold onto that thought until we get back to the room." He took off his jacket, covering her shoulders with it. "Although you look alluring in that wet dress, it's quite scandalous, my dear," he said with a lustful smirk.

Brie followed Sir, trusting he knew his way through the dark labyrinth of streets. When they finally arrived at the hotel, they were greeted by a sympathetic staff who quickly got towels for them and offered to bring up hot tea.

Sir thanked them, but assured the staff that the two of them would prefer to remain undisturbed. There were knowing glances amongst the hotel workers as Brie and Sir left for their room.

Brie began laughing when she saw herself in the mirror after taking off Sir's jacket. "I look like a stray cat, all soaking wet from the rain."

"I happen to prefer wet pussy," Sir said, coming up beside her. When he looked down at Brie, his expression suddenly changed. Sir brushed back the wet hair from her face and stared into her eyes as if seeing her for the first time. He leaned down to kiss her. "I love you, Brianna Renee Davis."

She smiled as she looked up at him, alarmed by the overpowering realization that her love for Sir knew no bounds.

I would do anything for him.

He caressed her cheek. "You're shivering, babygirl."

The truth was that she was trembling, overwhelmed by her love for her husband and Master.

"First things first, I need to get you out of that wet dress and into a hot bath," he ordered, picking her up and pressing her wet body against him. He twirled her around while droplets of water fell to the floor. "*Then* I will have my way with your body—again."

A Little Table Action

Before they left Venice, Sir took Brie to the charming *Ponte di Rialto*, a bridge that spanned the canal and was lined with little shops on either side, but these were different shops from the ones she was expecting.

Instead of kinky toys, there was an abundance of gold chains, sparkly jewels, and stylish fashion.

"You can choose anything you want, my gift to you."

She took his hand and grinned. "Then I choose you!"

Sir shook his head, a smile playing on his lips. "Since you already have me, why don't you choose something else you would enjoy."

Looking up and down the crowded bridge, Brie couldn't decide where to begin.

"Let's start on the left and make our way all the way around so you will have seen everything by the time you're done," Sir suggested, deftly moving Brie out of the path of a frowning individual who was bulling his way through the throng of people.

"You'll get there regardless if you push people out of

the way or not," Sir snarled at the man.

"Tourists," the man spat back angrily.

"People," Sir replied with conviction.

The man waved his hand in irritation as he pushed his way along, but managed to step out of the way of a little boy who had wandered into his path.

Brie looked up at Sir, grateful he was the kind of man who spoke his mind and that people listened to him—whether they wanted to or not.

"This first shop appears to have authentic Venetian glass," Sir told her. "Shall we pick a piece for our apartment?" Brie loved the idea and walked inside, instantly spying a piece that called to her. Picking up the unique blue and gold vase to admire, she blanched as soon as she saw the price and quickly set it back down.

Sir came up from behind and picked up the vase to look at the price. "That is a reasonable amount for glass blown by a true Venetian artisan. Should you find it cheaper, you would be looking at a fake." Brie took the vase from Sir to look at it again. He added, "I like this piece as well, if that helps with your decision."

She was pleased that he liked it. "If we both like this piece then it will have meaning to both of us in the years to come." Brie walked over to the shopkeeper and carefully handed her the vase. As the woman wrapped it, Sir took out his wallet and handed over several large bills.

"Now on to your next conquest."

Brie did a lot of window shopping, seeing many beautiful things, but not finding anything that stood out as something she would love to own. She knew Sir was getting a little frustrated when he said, "Nothing more?

We've passed more than twenty shops. What kind of woman are you?"

She laughed out loud. "I'm practical, Sir. I can't help it. I want something that I can't live without. Otherwise, it will just sit in a box or on a shelf gathering dust."

Sir kissed the top of her head. "While I do appreciate your way of thinking, it makes spoiling you rather difficult."

Knowing it was important to him that she pick something, Brie entered a shop of gold chains. The bright shiny color and sheer quantity of them was awe-inspiring. "Ooh…"

Brie touched the length of chains and smiled at the twinkling jewels on some of the necklaces, but what really set her heart aflutter was an intricate chain made for the ankle. She pointed it out to Sir.

He scoffed at the short chain. "You can have anything here—in fact, you can pick multiple things. Don't be shy, Brie."

"But Sir, all I want is this." She held up the delicate ankle bracelet. "Think how pretty it will look when I'm in compromising positions."

He raised an eyebrow. "Oh hell, that's the last thing I need to think about right now…" He turned away from the shopkeeper to hide his growing erection. Brie smiled as he pretended to look at the prices of the longer chains while he regained his composure. Once focused, Sir turned to face her again. "So the ankle bracelet it is."

He took it from her and quickly paid the man.

Instead of wrapping it up, Sir insisted on putting it around her ankle in the shop. He knelt on the floor and grasped her ankle firmly. She felt pleasant tingles as he attached the chain, but her heart skipped a beat when he looked up at her lustfully.

Sir stood back up grinning, confident in the knowledge he'd returned the favor by stirring her arousal.

"I think I'm done shopping now," Brie blurted.

"I am too," he agreed. "Shall we find a nice private table for lunch before we go?"

"That would be absolutely lovely, Sir."

They walked out of the shop like any other vanilla couple enjoying the famous bridge, but the only thing on Brie's mind was the gold chain around her ankle and how it would look with her legs in the air.

She was surprised when Sir took her to a busy restaurant next to the canal, but noticed he handed the host a tip before they were taken to the back of the small restaurant to a private table in a little cove area.

Sir pulled out the chair for Brie and moved his chair next to hers before sitting down. He examined the tablecloth thoughtfully and stated, "Not quite long enough, but we will have to make do."

Brie smiled, understanding his meaning.

"*Grazie*," Sir told the waiter when he handed over a menu. He ordered for both of them, picking a local seafood dish for himself and a caprese salad for her, along with a bottle of wine.

"It's such a shame you dislike seafood, my dear. You're missing out on some of the best."

Brie grinned, holding up her glass of wine. "Actually, I enjoy 'sea'men. It has a saltiness similar to seafood, but features an extra tanginess I crave." She took a sip and added quietly, "Especially yours."

"Naughty girl," he reprimanded.

Rather than have Brie sneak under the table and take him in her mouth, Sir instructed her to lay her napkin over her lap while he did the same. "Adjust your clothing appropriately to allow for access," he instructed.

With a little maneuvering, she had her panties pulled down just above where the hem of the skirt ended and hiked the material of her skirt up on his side. The side facing the fellow restaurateurs would not reveal anything out of the ordinary.

"Very good," he said, when he too had made the needed adjustments. "Scoot closer to the table so we can enjoy our lunch."

Once settled, Brie felt Sir's hand sneak under her napkin to her exposed mound. He ran his finger between the soft folds of her pussy, lightly stroking her clit. She bit her lip, enjoying his intimate touch far too much.

In return, she slowly reached under his napkin and grasped his already erect shaft. Brie looked out over the crowd of customers as she sipped her wine leisurely and stroked her Master's cock.

The waiter returned with their meals. Neither stopped their intimate caresses while the server asked if they wanted extra parmesan.

"Certainly," Sir answered.

Sir flicked her clit and then slowly sank a finger inside as the waiter began grating the cheese over Brie's plate. "Just tell me when, *signora*."

Brie stifled a moan as Sir traveled deeper, her whole

body focused on that one wicked finger.

"*Signora?*" the server questioned.

Brie blushed when she looked up at him and then down at her plate where there was a small mountain of grated cheese growing. "When," she said meekly and then added, "I have a thing for cheese."

Sir replied with a smirk, "As do I."

The waiter nodded and started vigorously grating the cheese over Sir's dish, determined to give him an equal amount. "*Bene*," Sir replied quickly. "Although I enjoy a good Italian cheese, I prefer to actually taste the meal."

"Very good, *signore*," the man replied, eyeing Brie's plate with amusement as he left.

Once the server was out of hearing range, Sir asked her, "A little distracted, were we?"

Brie giggled as she stared at the mound of parmesan. "Just a little, Sir."

"*Bene.*" Sir began teasing her clit again while he took his fork and twirled the thick noodles, taking a bite and vocalizing his pleasure. "Authentic *Bigoli in salsa* is a rare treat."

She pursed her lips, trying to concentrate on his shaft while she took a spoonful of the grated cheese and popped it in her mouth. "Yum, cheese."

Brie took a sharp intake of breath as he fingered her more vigorously. She responded by dragging her nails against his shaft as if they were her teeth. Sir stopped mid-bite, quite frozen. He put his fork down, looking straight ahead.

Brie was feeling immensely powerful getting that kind of reaction from him. She brushed away a section of the grated cheese to cut into the fresh mozzarella and tomato, picking up the bite-sized piece. As she closed her lips around it, Sir started stroking her pussy as if he were licking her. Brie forced herself to chew, moaning softly when the waiter returned to ask if everything was satisfactory.

"We're quite satisfied," Sir replied.

"Is the parmesan to your liking, *signora?*" he asked when he noticed she'd only had one bite of her salad.

"Oh yes," she assured him. "I like to savor my meals."

"Understood," he said, glancing at Sir.

Brie wondered if he had figured out what was going on under the table with their hands "resting" on each other.

After he left, Sir picked up his fork and re-twirled his pasta, looking at her lustfully as he bit down on it. She watched his sexy lips as he chewed, imagining those lips on her.

"Eat, my dear. I want you well fed before I devour you."

She squeaked when he started back up, hitting just the right spot to set her entire nether regions ablaze. It took concentration to eat another bite, but while she chewed she ramped up her own teasing, lightly fingering his frenulum as if it were her tongue.

They continued their meal, completely enraptured with each other. Brie could have been eating fish and she wouldn't have noticed at that point. The best part was that the hotel room was not far away. All their teasing at lunch would result in heavenly release for dessert.

When their meal was done, Sir took out the kerchief from his pocket and handed it to her.

"Sir?"

"A substitute for a towel."

"Ah…" She dried herself off inconspicuously and pulled her skirt down before lifting her napkin from her lap to dab at her lips demurely.

Sir took his kerchief from her and brought it to his lips with a twinkle in his eye before stuffing it back into his breast pocket.

The waiter returned. "Any dessert, *signora*?"

"No, thank you. We have dessert waiting for us back at the hotel."

"Of course." He bowed to her before leaving the check on the table and gathering their plates. "I hope you enjoyed the meal."

"It was quiet delicious."

"Wonderful. Please come visit us again."

"I hope to every time we visit," she confessed.

"Wonderful." He gave a final bow to Sir before walking away.

Sir stood up and took Brie's hand, leading her out of the restaurant. She noticed he walked a little more stiffly than normal, which warmed her subbie heart.

Leaving the hotel room, much less Venice, was hard because Brie was totally in love with the romance of the city.

When Sir saw her mournful look he teased, "Would you rather I cancel my other plans?"

"No, of course not. I just can't imagine anything being as wonderful as this." She wrapped her arms around his waist. "This place seems to bring out the sexy animal in you."

His kissed her forehead. "I assure you it has nothing to do with Venice and everything to do with you."

She stood on her tiptoes to kiss him on the lips. "Prince Charming in Dom's clothing."

Sir fisted her hair and pulled her head back to kiss her more forcibly, letting her feel his power over her. "But a Dom to the core, never forget that." He kissed her hard before letting go.

Brie purred, "I do love that about you."

He threw the overnight bag over his shoulder. "Are you ready to live out a fantasy of mine?"

A huge grin spread across Brie's face. "Absolutely, Sir. Any hint as to what it might be?"

He surprised her when he actually provided one. "Think privacy."

"That's not much to go on."

"But it's more than you knew a second ago," he replied with a smirk.

Brie laughed as she took his hand and walked out of the hotel room, looking back wistfully.

Goodbye, my Fertility Room of Love…

Heaven on Earth

To Brie's surprise, Sir had arranged a private jet for them. As he helped her up the steps onto the small plane, a young, dark-skinned woman with black hair accented with a tropical flower greeted them inside.

"Hello, Mr. and Mrs. Davis. My name is Talei. May I offer you a drink while we wait to take off?"

"A dirty martini for me, and you?" Sir asked Brie.

She was riding high on love and everything Italian, not quite ready to leave it yet, so she asked for a glass of red wine. Dying to know where they were headed, and certain the stewardess was another clue, Brie told her, "Talei is such a beautiful name."

"Thank you, my father gave it to me."

"What does it mean?"

"Precious one."

"That's so sweet."

With that little bit of information, Brie got out her phone and googled baby names to discover the origin of it. What popped up thrilled her. She put her phone down and took a sip of wine, looking at Sir knowingly.

"What's the Cheshire cat grin for?" he asked.

"I take it this will be a long flight."

Sir raised an eyebrow, pleased by her question. "How long do you think?"

Brie picked up her phone again and typed in the travel time by air. "I'm thinking maybe twenty-two hours. Am I right?"

Instead of answering her, he stated matter-of-factly, "This jet is equipped with a comfortable bed."

"I'm glad, because I will need my beauty sleep to properly show off the sexy bikini I brought with me."

Not budging an inch, he replied, "I'm unsure how much rest you will be getting on that bed."

Since he wasn't giving out any more hints, Brie returned to her phone, googling popular foods of the region. There was one popular dish that involved a pit, hot rocks, and banana leaves. "So Sir, I'm pretty sure most of the food there will be seafood, but I'm hoping to try the *Lovo*. It sounds interesting."

The glint in Sir's eyes let her know she'd guessed correctly. "I believe a traditional *Lovo* can be arranged."

Brie jumped up from her seat and climbed onto Sir's lap. "How exciting! I've always wanted to travel somewhere tropical."

His low chuckle delighted her as he pulled her tight against him.

"The only thing I'm not quite sure about is how your fantasy is involved."

He picked up his martini with one hand while still holding her, giving her a mischievous wink as he downed his drink.

Brie laughed, conceding defeat. "I truly have a love/hate relationship with your cruelty, Sir. But still, we're going to Fiji!"

"Yes, but it won't be anytime soon unless you buckle yourself in. Talei just signaled they are ready for takeoff."

Brie gave him a quick peck on the cheek before sitting back down and adjusting her buckle. She looked out the window and took in a deep breath, hardly able to contain herself.

Fiji!

What fantasy would they be playing out together in that exotic location?

When they stepped off the plane after the long trip, feeling deliciously stated, Brie was hit by the intense blue waters and beautiful variants of greens of the tropical vegetation. It was far more beautiful than the pictures she'd seen of the islands. They didn't do Fiji any justice.

Brie was taking it all in when Sir surprised her by directing her to a smaller plane with pontoons. "This is not our destination," he informed her.

Although she would have appreciated more time to stretch her legs, she got onto the tiny plane, excited to see what a puddle jumper would be like.

Sir clasped her hand as they took off, the look in his eye holding excitement she didn't normally see. It gave him a boyish charm that made her love him that much harder.

As they flew past many small islands, Sir yelled over the roar of the engine, "I had to have everything shipped—from food and water, to the little extras."

"Little extras?"

He only laughed, looking out the window with an infectious grin on his face.

Sir never let his inner child out—whatever this fantasy was, it had the power to bring out that side of him. Brie loved seeing it.

The pilot pointed to a tiny island coming into view.

Sir nodded and looked at Brie, his eyes sparkling mischievously. "That's our island."

"What?" She pressed her head against the glass to get a better look.

It was a small island covered in trees, with white beaches, surrounded by insanely blue waters. A lone isle in the middle of all that blue. Rather than the luxurious resort Brie had expected, they were going to stay on a deserted island.

Sir explained as the small plane began its descent, "I thought to myself, 'Where would I go and what would I do if I could go anywhere for our honeymoon?' Venice was for you, but this..." he pointed to the island, "this is for me."

Brie held onto Sir tightly as the plane skidded across the water and slowly made its way closer to shore.

"Do you remember when we visited my father's little island?"

"I do, Sir. I have so many wonderful memories of that day."

He leaned over her to open the door on her side.

"Do you remember how we got onto that island?"

"Yes, you chased me."

"Well, there is only one way off this plane, so I suggest you started undressing."

"I don't have my bikini on," she giggled, thinking he was only kidding.

"You won't be needing it," he answered. "Let's see if you can escape my clutches this time."

Brie's eyes widened as she saw Sir start to undress. Without thinking, she started ripping off her top. "But shouldn't I bring them with me?" she blurted.

"Only if your clothes won't slow you down."

There was no way she could swim faster than Sir with clothes, so she tossed her shoes off, undid her bra and shimmied out of her skirt and panties. Sir was already taking off his belt. With no time to lose, Brie positioned herself at the edge of the doorway and launched herself into the water to avoid the pontoon below.

Brie started swimming with long, controlled strokes, spying an opening in the vegetation on shore. Her plan was to get lost in the foliage and hide from him.

Her heart fluttered when she heard him hit the water, knowing she'd have to swim even faster. The adrenaline kicked in and she picked up steam, nearly getting to the edge of the beach.

Her illusions of escape were quickly squashed, however, when she felt Sir grab her ankles. Struggling proved pointless as he easily pulled her into him with those strong arms.

Sir wrapped one around her and dragged her onto

the shore, and then collapsed on top of her body, looking down at her with devilish eyes as they both panted, catching their breath.

"I saw your ship go down, and when I saw you struggling I swam out to recue you."

"My hero," she smiled up at him.

"As the only survivor of the shipwreck, you're fortunate to have ended up here. Welcome to my island."

"Your island?" she questioned.

"Yes, I have been waiting to unleash my deviant passions on a woman. And here you are…"

Brie wasn't sure where his roleplaying was headed, but she definitely wanted Sir to unleash his passions all over her.

Before Brie could react, Sir leaned down and kissed her, plundering her mouth with the salty taste of the ocean as his tongue darted between her lips. As much as she wanted to resist for the sake of his roleplay, she completely melted into that kiss, wrapping her arms around him.

Sir pressed her into the sandy beach with his weight as the water lapped against their naked bodies. "You're mine now," he stated possessively.

"Bound by honor to repay you for saving my life," she replied.

"Oh, the things I have planned for this naked body of yours…" he growled lustfully. "But first I will show you my island."

Sir stood up and lorded over her in all his naked glory as he brushed the sand off. "Come," he commanded in an authoritative voice, pulling her up and swiping his hand against her skin to remove the gritty sand. But his swipes were slow and sensual, lingering overly long on her intimate parts.

Once he was finished wiping her off, Sir took Brie's hand in his and led her through the opening in the vegetation Brie had spied earlier. It turned out to be a small path.

What had made it? she wondered.

Brie looked up at the canopy of trees above her, seeing several different kinds of birds flying from limb to limb.

The crowded forest of trees and vegetation eventually opened up to a large clearing. Here in the middle of nowhere, a miniature home had been constructed. The front of it was made of glass. Inside she could see a sizeable bed, tiny kitchen, a freestanding tub and, to her great delight, a tantra chair set in the middle of the one-room structure.

Brie shook her head in amazement as he opened the door and escorted her inside. "I have everything we need," he stated proudly. "There's a full tank of water in the back, enough for a week, and…" He opened the cupboards in the miniature kitchen. "A fully stocked pantry."

"How?"

He raised an eyebrow. "I have connections."

She glanced around the tiny but impressive living space. "Very important connections, by the looks of it."

"That's not the best part." Sir pointed to the sizeable bed. On it sat a large leather bag. "Those are special tools I requested." He ran his fingers over the length of her arm, causing goosebumps to follow. "Tools I plan to use on you."

Brie felt a pleasant chill run through her. "What kind of tools?"

"The kind that makes a young woman scream. On this island no one will hear you."

She looked at him warily. "Happy screams, I hope."

Sir only smiled. The glint in his eye made her uncertain.

He sniffed the air and grinned. "I want to show you something else. It demonstrates how in sync I am with your needs."

Brie followed him out of the miniature home and they walked to the far end of the clearing where smoke was rising from under banana leaves carefully laid on the ground. The odor coming from it had Brie's mouth watering.

"Traditional *Lovo* is being prepared for us."

"No way!" Brie dropped to her knees and took in a long sniff. The smell of cooking meats and root vegetables filled her senses, and her stomach responded by growling loudly. "How long will it take before it's ready?"

"It should be cooked by the time I've fully enjoyed your fine ass."

Brie looked up at him from her impromptu kneeling position, and batted her eyes innocently. "My ass?"

"Yes, I'm going to thoroughly fuck that pink rosette of yours."

Sir picked her up and threw her over his shoulder. She looked down and couldn't help noticing how incredibly sexy his butt was. Without thinking, she grabbed his ass cheeks with both hands.

"Hands off," he commanded, a hint of amusement in his voice.

When they entered the tiny home, Sir headed straight for the far-off corner where a small open shower was waiting for them. He turned on the water while she was still bent over his shoulder.

He lifted her off and set her directly under the stream of water.

"It's too cold!" she screamed, trying to escape the icy water, but he held her firmly under the showerhead. "When you're on a deserted island you don't get the luxury of being picky." He added as a side comment, "Would you rather have the sand that remains between your legs 'add' to your experience?"

Brie shook her head violently, choosing to stay still as he finished rinsing all the grit off. Once he was satisfied she was free of sand, he ordered her to dry as he rinsed himself off.

"Lay yourself over the high end of the chair, facing the glass."

Brie lay on the rounded end of the tantra chair, appreciating the caress of the soft leather against her stomach. Sir had yet to fuck her ass since their honeymoon began—every encounter being centered on sperm meeting egg. It almost seemed wicked and self-indulgent to be having anal sex. Knowing it was a "waste" of his seed seemed to make it all that much hotter.

Sir toweled off and walked over to her, spreading her ass cheeks to inspect the tight hole he was about to penetrate. "Put your hands behind your back."

Brie did as she was told and felt the familiar constraint of leather cuffs as he secured them around her wrists. She smiled to herself when she heard the satisfying clanking sound as he grabbed the connecting metal chain with one hand and pulled back on it. "For better leverage."

Brie was excited; her whole body was trembling in anticipation of his hard shaft breaching her tight hole.

She moaned softly when she felt his fingers glide over her rosette with slippery lubricant. He also applied some to his shaft before grabbing onto her buttocks with both hands, separating her ass cheeks with his thumbs. "There it is, just waiting for me to fuck it."

Brie said nothing as she stared ahead, longing to be taken.

"Tell me what you want," Sir demanded.

Brie paused a few seconds before answering, thinking back on their very first encounter together. "I want to be taken by you."

"Describe what you want."

"I want you to fuck my ass with your hard cock."

"Do you want it gentle or rough?"

She paused for dramatic effect. "Whatever is your pleasure."

"I think it pleases me to give you both…"

Her heart raced as he slid his hard shaft over her sensitive hole, physically stating his intentions as he teased her with the head of his cock.

Brie closed her eyes, liking the fact he held back, drawing out the moment of penetration. It was unbearably delicious.

Brie bit her bottom lip as he began to push, her muscles initially resisting the penetration even though she wanted him. However, she liked that aspect about anal intercourse—the fact she had to consciously surrender her mind and body to his will.

Sir made a guttural sound when his cock finally slipped inside. Brie moaned in response, loving the pleasurable ache his hard shaft caused, stretching her as he continued to push deeper.

"Fuck, that feels good…"

"Too good," she purred.

He stopped. "Do you want me to pull out then?"

"No," she begged, "Please keep going."

"You *are* a dirty girl. I saw that in you the first time we met," he replied, grabbing onto her cuffs for leverage as he pushed deeper.

Her body finally opened up to him, allowing him greater depth which they both desired. He began to caress her tight ass with long, solid strokes.

"Oh, that feels…so…so…goooooood," she cried.

Sir's groan let her know he felt the same, but he wasn't satisfied for very long. Brie felt a drip of extra lubricant around the stretched skin of her opening. "That's right, girl, I'm about to switch gears."

Brie looked back at him flirtatiously. "I like it rough."

"Of course you do," he answered with a wicked grin, taking a new grip of the cuffs and pulling her upper torso off the tantra chair. "Now that your body is prepared I will show no restraint."

Brie held her breath as Sir began to pound her with

his cock. He kept with the long strokes, but they came at a much faster pace and far deeper. She had to close her eyes and concentrate to prevent her body from resisting the forceful onslaught.

"Breathe," he commanded.

She appreciated the reminder and let her breath go, refilling her lungs with the tropical air.

Sir ramped up, holding onto the cuffs firmly as he fucked her like a jackhammer.

Skin slapping against skin filled the room as his shaft dominated her ass. Just when she didn't think she could take any more, he stopped and began rolling his hips, every stroke as deep as he could force it.

Brie felt her pussy began to pulse. "Oh God, I'm about to come."

"I want to feel it."

Her ass muscles tensed unbearably around his cock just before her release. She cried out as her climax flooded over her—Sir's low grunts enhancing her orgasm.

"That was a good one. Shall we go for another?"

"If it pleases you," she answered with a playful backwards glance.

In answer, Sir held the cuffs tight as he thrust his shaft in again. Brie cried out, tensing from the power of the stroke but her body quickly relaxed, leaving her begging for more.

"So you like a good ass fucking," he commented with satisfaction.

"I love the feeling of total possession."

"Good, because I plan to climax in your ass as you

come."

She moaned breathlessly. "Just thinking about that makes my pussy quiver with pleasure."

"I'm feeling generous today and will not make you wait." With that, he held onto the cuffs with one hand while grabbing the flesh of her ass with the other. The pounding began, not only taking her breath away but all her other senses too.

His shaft filled her world.

When her second orgasm hit, Sir stopped thrusting to enjoy the rhythmic contractions of her strong inner muscles before he allowed his own release. Brie screamed out in passion when his cock seemed to grow even bigger just before he thrust deep and warm come filled her ass.

Brie closed her eyes, not wanting to miss the final shudder of his climax—it was something she found extremely sexy. "Why does that feel so good?" she mused as he pulled out and slapped her on the ass.

"It's simple," he answered. "Your body was meant for my pleasure, making every part of you *my* domain to dominate. It's only natural you would enjoy it."

"Do you say that to all the girls?"

Sir leaned in close. "No. Only to you, wife."

Brie purred as Sir unbuckled her cuffs and lifted her up, carrying her to the bed. She loved the rush of endorphins that came after such intense play, but she loved his aftercare equally as much.

Sir nuzzled her ear as he lightly caressed her back with gentle hands. "Did you like playing out my fantasy?"

"Very much…although I couldn't pretend not to want you," she giggled. "I'm sorry if you were hoping for that."

"I didn't need a reluctant captive."

She turned her head toward him and smiled. "This was one time I couldn't even fake it."

He caressed her cheek. "You are my anchor, baby-girl. I find myself feeling hope for the future without my normal reservations. To be honest, it is a strange feeling for me."

She was amused and asked why.

"You know me. I'm always calculating the consequences of my decisions. I should be concerned about becoming a father, and yet…I feel nothing but peace. It's unnatural."

She laughed. "Actually, Sir, it's not. That's how I've lived my whole life and I have zero complaints about how my life's turned out."

He smacked her bottom playfully. "I still think you were a fool to offer me your collar. I'm a complicated beast with demons that still play out in my head."

Brie knew the beast reference was in relation to his mother—a death he had yet to reconcile.

With loving hands, she cradled his face. "You're not a beast. You are a man with a complicated past who is fortunate to have a woman who loves you completely. A woman who would do anything for you."

"Although I must repeat that you were foolish, I have benefitted greatly from your mistake."

"No mistake, Sir. It was my destiny—and yours."

He sighed in frustration. "There it is again. That

quandary whether we decide our fates or some divine power from above influences our lives. I find the latter to be disturbing, despite Marquis' certainty that God exists."

"You know…I've always found Marquis Gray's faith inspiring. If someone that intelligent and independent believes in a higher power, it makes me wonder if he might be right."

Sir snorted. "Marquis is a mystery."

"But you admire him, Sir," Brie stated confidently.

Sir frowned. "Let's just say that there are aspects of the man that I deeply respect. However, his belief in God is not one of them."

"Because?"

Sir snarled, "Believing in God takes my will out of the equation. I don't like the idea of being someone else's puppet."

Brie tilted her head, excited by a new train of thought inspired by their conversation. "What if… it's more like a Dominant and submissive dynamic? The Dom has no power over the submissive unless he or she allows it."

"Oh hell, woman. I did not come to this private island to discuss theology with you. I came here to do one thing and one thing only."

"And that is?"

"To fuck your ever-lovin' brains out."

Brie laughed. In one fell swoop Sir had gone from a serious discussion to needing to bang her again.

A change in direction of the breeze sent the delicious aroma of cooking *Lovo* drifting into the miniature home. Brie's stomach growled in response and would not stop.

She blushed a deep red as she cradled her tummy.

"I suppose we should eat before I play with you again," he conceded. "I need sustenance in order to recharge my sperm production. No point in sending the boys in unless they're up for the job."

Brie burst out laughing again as she made her way to the shower. Soon she was whimpering, however, as the cold water hit her sweaty skin. She rinsed off as quickly as possible to escape the icy cold. After she toweled off, she glanced around the room. "Did you bring our clothes, Sir?"

He chuckled, not answering her until he dried off himself.

"We have no clothes on the isle."

"Why?"

"My fantasy is to be stranded on this island naked and alone with you. Like Adam and Eve… A little more civilized with modern conveniences, but a little more brutish in the way we approach our procreation."

"Oh, I like that analogy!" she said, grinning. "The only two people on earth—our sole purpose is making love to create a child."

Sir scrubbed his wet hair vigorously with the towel, looking at her all disheveled and devastatingly cute when he informed her, "The plane won't arrive again for another six days."

"A full week of purposeful debauchery…"

"Truly heaven on earth, wouldn't you agree?" he asked with a devilish grin.

Her stomach growled in answer.

Sir pinched her bare ass as they walked toward the

smoldering fire. "Let's get you fed so I can ravage that delectable body repeatedly."

He pulled back the large banana leaves and placed them on the sand. Using a shovel, he removed the hot rocks and pulled back more banana leaves until he came to a layer of vegetables. Using tongs, he placed them on the largest banana leaf.

Underneath the layer of veggies were large pieces of meat, both pork and chicken.

"As is tradition, we eat with our fingers," Sir stated.

In her hunger Brie immediately grabbed a yam. "Hot, hot, hot!" she cried, dropping it on the ground as she stuck her fingers in her mouth.

"Have you never played hot potato before?" Sir teased.

He gingerly took a piece of chicken, handling only the edges as he took the first bite. "Oh hell, that's good."

Sir held it out for her to take a bite. She took her fingers out of her mouth and bit into the piece. It was tender and delicious, perfectly flavored by the smoke. She took another bigger bite and smiled at him.

Sir handed her the chicken and took a hunk of pork.

They sat there naked, eating with their bare hands as they nibbled on each other's food. It couldn't have been more primal or romantic.

By the end of the meal, Brie was covered in sticky goodness as she eagerly licked her hands. Somehow, Sir had managed to stay clean.

She looked at him in disbelief. "How is that even possible?"

"I'm not quite as enthusiastic as you when I eat."

"I'm glad this isn't our first date. I might have scared you away with my appetite."

"I never shy away from a woman with a healthy appetite, as long as she is willing to clean up afterwards."

Brie frowned. "Another cold shower?"

"No," he said with a twinkle in his eye. "Stay here while I ready your bath." He grabbed the shovel and scooped up some of the hot stones, carrying them into the house. Once it was ready he came back to collect her. "Warm bath, Mrs. Davis?"

Brie took his hand and stood up. "Oh, that sounds heavenly, Mr. Davis."

When they entered the little house, he told her to test the water.

Brie approached the unusual tub. It was made of frosted blue glass held up by a dark metal frame that resembled bare trees branches with a skyline of pine trees in the background. She was uncertain why they were pine and not palms, but it was simply magnificent. A piece of functional art that had somehow found its way to the deserted isle.

Brie stooped to run her fingers in the water. It was perfectly warm and she purred, "It's just the right temperature."

"Good," He walked over and helped Brie step into the tub. She settled down into the warm water and moaned in pure bliss as it enveloped her.

Sir picked up a pitcher beside the tub and pushed it under the water, filling it up. "Have you ever had your hair washed by a man before?"

"No, but it's always been a dream of mine."

"Lay your head back then," he commanded gently. Brie felt warm, ticklish chills as the water cascaded over her hair and down her back. Sir took his time, using several pitchers to make sure her hair was thoroughly wet.

He leaned over to give Brie a kiss before getting the shampoo. Her entire scalp tingled with pleasure as he massaged the lather in. It was like a delicious skin-gasm, making her body pleasantly weak from the sensual stimulation.

"Have you ever thought of doing this for a living, Sir? I'm positive many women would pay to experience such lavish treatment."

He chuckled lightly as he got the pitcher again, beginning the slow process of rinsing her hair clean. She shivered in delight as the water flowed down, seducing her with its liquid caress.

When he was done, he took a fluffy towel and wrapped her hair in it. "For now, I want you to relax and enjoy your bath. You can join me outside when the water gets cold." She watched him walk away from her, admiring his fine, manly ass.

Brie sighed as she lay in the tub, smiling so hard her cheeks hurt. Her stomach was full, her body satisfied, her soul content, and her heart overflowing with love.

Truly this was heaven on earth...

Buried Treasure

S ir had tied Brie up tight in jute. She was hanging naked between the trunks of two palms that leaned toward each other. He'd left her there to admire the gorgeous sunset while he returned to the miniature home to select a new toy to play with.

Tonight was to be their last on the isle.

Early tomorrow morning the plane was coming back to whisk them away from their private heaven. Knowing they were going had Brie feeling melancholy, especially when the waves were calling so sweetly to her.

How can I ever leave this?

She wished they were self-made billionaires who could travel the world and play without concerning themselves with deadlines and the pressures of work. But then she had to laugh; neither Sir nor she were made for such a passive life. Although this escape from reality had been absolutely divine, it was the daily challenges and hard-fought successes that had honed Brie into who she was.

To wish away the things that fortified her was silly.

So she savored the beauty of their last sunset as she lay suspended in rope, knowing this memory would last her lifetime.

Sir returned to her with a piece of old parchment rolled up and secured with a wax seal. He laid it on the sand in front of her.

"What's that?"

He answered with a wink. "That, babygirl, is a treasure map."

She smiled, thrilled by the prospect. "What kind of treasure, Master?"

"It's up to you to uncover it and find out, but not before I partake of your perfectly positioned body." He ran his hand over her bare mound. "I'm going to give the rope just enough slack to enjoy myself."

Brie watched as he skillfully adjusted the ropes. He did not have the quick hands of Tono, but he certainly knew his way around rope.

Aware of her love of the art of kinbaku, he had taken the time to learn its intricacies from the Kinbaku Master himself. Sir didn't want her to miss any experience he knew she enjoyed.

The difference, however, lay in how he used the rope. With Sir, it was less about letting her fly and more about enhancing their sexual encounters. Brie smiled to herself, gratified that Sir had taken his duty seriously and been quite creative in the different ways he found to procreate.

Her pussy had been well used over the course of the week.

Sir stood in front of her, presenting her with his

cock. "You know what to do, wife."

"With pleasure, husband." Brie opened her mouth and took his hardening cock between her warm lips. He sucked in his breath as she started to tease his manhood with her teeth.

"You know what that does to me," he growled under his breath.

She smiled but did not disengage her mouth. Yes, she knew him well and enjoyed the occasional tease, but she returned to sucking and licking, not wanting to lose this chance to feel his cock inside her as the sun disappeared over the horizon.

He moved away from her mouth when he was satisfied, kneeling down between her open legs to position his tongue. "It's only fair…" he murmured lustfully as he took a lick. He groaned again as he took another long lick, stimulating her clit as he caressed her outer folds with his fingers.

"I've always admired your beautiful pussy. When you came back to class after your first waxing to show off Sting's work, I had to suppress the urge to christen it with my come right there in front of the panel."

"You know I would have welcomed your advances."

He snorted in amusement, his warm breath caressing the delicate skin of her sex. "Oh yes, that would certainly have been well received by the other trainers."

Sir placed his hand possessively on her pussy as he stood up to position himself to take her. Grabbing onto the ropes, he started her swinging. Brie felt the barest hint of his hard shaft touch her sex. Each consecutive swing brought her closer to gratification, but she was helplessly bound and could only wait until he deemed it time.

Sir controlled her motion. He knew the power of expectancy and was a Master at making her wait for satisfaction. When the head of his shaft finally grazed her wet pussy, she moaned loudly.

"Throw your head back. I want you to watch the sun disappear as I stroke your pussy to climax."

Brie stared out at the ocean, watching the sun slowly sink down past the horizon. Sir used the rope to control his thrusts. They were quick, diminutive movements, the head of his shaft rubbing against her g-spot continuously.

The moment the sun disappeared her body exploded in a continuous wave of ecstasy. They both cried out in pleasure, filling the night air with their carnal passion.

Sir unfurled a blanket afterward and laid it underneath her. He then lit four torches, setting them around her in the sand before he began the task of lowering her down to the blanket and untying the knots.

He rubbed her skin tenderly as he cradled her in the firelight. "The rope marks are attractive on you."

She glided her finger over one on her arm and purred. "They feel good, too. Thank you, Sir." Brie smiled at Sir, but her eyes kept glancing over to the parchment.

"It's killing you, isn't it?"

She giggled.

"You're dying to know what it is."

"Of course I am—you know me."

His laughter was deep and alluring. Sir picked up the

parchment and placed it in her hands. "I give you permission to break the seal, but—" She immediately started to bend the wax when he cautioned her, "Before you do you need to understand my rules."

"What rules?"

"You will find a treasure based on this map. There are several markers along the way. I expect you to collect each one and will give you a set amount of time, each increasingly longer, for every marker you find. If you fail to produce a marker within the allotted time, you will be punished."

"Punished, Sir?"

He smiled as he looked down at a pocket watch in his hand. "If you agree to these rules, you may break the seal."

Brie laughed nervously as she hesitantly broke the wax seal. She was far too curious to let the threat of punishment stop her from finding out what surprise awaited her at the end of the hunt. Brie unrolled the stiff paper and looked over the map Sir had drawn.

Glancing at him in concern, she asked, "You want me to do this in the dark?"

He looked at his watch again and winked at her. "You have ten minutes to find the first marker."

Brie squeaked when he produced a paddle from behind his back. She quickly studied the map again, feeling confident she needed to head down the edge of the beach. She grabbed one of the torches, grasping the handle to pull it out of the sand. Her heart was already racing.

Failure is not an option!

She ran down the beach. Once she reached the water, she glanced at the map again, noting something that looked like tiny lines crisscrossing each other. She had no idea what Sir meant by it, but saw something dark up ahead. As she approached the mysterious mass, she lifted her torch and realized it was simply an old fisherman's net. She planted the torch into the sand and hoisted up the wet material. Underneath she found a gold coin shining brightly up at her. Bringing it next to the light of the torch, she saw that it had a small "p" stamped on it.

She hurried back to Sir, formally presenting the coin to him on her knees.

"Very good, téa, but I made the first one easy for you."

She stood up and smiled proudly.

"You'd better start looking. You've already wasted fifteen seconds."

Brie frowned, realizing that she'd been foolish to stand there. She quickly retraced her steps to the first marker and checked over her map again. Ahead was an outcropping of rocks she would have to navigate with bare feet. With no time to spare, she successfully traversed them looking for what appeared to be a tide pool. Unfortunately there were several, but she knew she'd found the right one when a flash of gold glinted in the water. Brie balanced herself on the lip of the rock as she squatted to scoop it out of the water. This coin had a small "e" stamped on it. Seeing they were different made Brie wonder if it would eventually spell out a word.

Not having time to contemplate, she started back towards Sir but began bolting when she heard him count down. "Three…two…one…"

Out of breath, she threw the coin to him as she ran up.

Sir let it fall to the ground at his feet, unimpressed. "You must present the coin, téa."

Knowing she had failed and must be punished, Brie dutifully knelt down on her knees and picked up the coin, presenting it to him with submissive grace.

"You're late."

She bowed her head. "I know, Master."

"Put down the torch, and lean against the tree for your punishment."

Brie closed her eyes as she pressed herself against the trunk of the tree.

"Why are you being punished, téa?" he asked playfully.

"I failed to return the marker to you in time."

"Exactly." Sir stood behind her and cupped his hand on her right buttock. "For the first offense, you will receive six swats." His hand traveled leisurely over to her left ass cheek for emphasis. "Three for each buttock."

The first swat shocked her with the sting of it, but the pain soon dissipated into a delicious warm feeling that spread out from the area. He smacked the other cheek with the same powerful stroke and she groaned in both pleasure and pain. By the time he was done, her butt was warm and tender from his focused attention.

"Next time it will be ten," he warned.

Not needing any more incentive, she hurried back to the rocks and studied the map. It appeared there was a tiny clearing with a misshapen circle in the dark vegetation on the far side of the tide pools.

As Brie pushed her way through the lush foliage, she was reminded of her paddling and rubbed the tender area with a smile. Playful punishment certainly was a turn-on for her.

She had to stop several times, blocked by thick vines, but she eventually found her way to the small clearing and saw the basketball-sized rock directly in the middle that matched Sir's drawing. She tried to lift the stone with one hand, but found it much too heavy.

She quickly propped the torch and push the small boulder over, but was disappointed not to see a coin underneath. She looked all around the edges of the clearing, knowing time was ticking.

Crap!

Looking back at the ground, she noticed freshly disturbed sand. Realizing Sir must have buried the coin, Brie began digging furiously. With adrenaline kicking in, she clawed at the sand and was finally rewarded with another coin with a small "o" stamped on it.

She grabbed her torch and raced back to Sir, who had already started counting down and was at ten.

Brie dropped to her knees and held up the coin to him.

"Well done," he said, sounding impressed.

Rather than wasting time basking in his praise, she stood up and gave him a quick bow before heading out. Returning to the clearing, she glanced at the map. To her delight, the next marker was somewhere at the house which was only a short walk from where she stood. She made her way through the dark foliage, following the light glowing from inside the small building.

The question was where he had hidden it because Sir had only drawn the miniature house. It could be anywhere in or around the building.

As soon as Brie broke through to the clearing she started searching around the outside of the little home, certain that Sir had made it a challenging find. After a thorough check, she entered the room and started digging through the cupboards. When that yielded nothing, she glanced around the room nervously. She'd already used up so much time…

Brie heard him start the countdown at twenty. She spied the tool bag Sir had left on the counter and started throwing his instruments out haphazardly. Finally, in desperation she dumped everything out of the bag but did not find the marker. She happened to glance at the bed…and there it was. The gold coin sitting in plain sight.

She roared in frustration and ran to pick it up. It was stamped with a small "h". She ran for all she was worth, sliding to a kneel at his feet and holding the coin up, panting heavily.

"…zero. That was as under the wire as you can get."

She nodded, still unable to speak.

Sir took the coin from her. "The last marker," he stated. "Do you know what they mean, téa?"

Brie looked up at him. "May I have them, Master?"

Sir opened his palm and she took them from him. Laying the coins on the sand, she realized there was only one word it could be. She arranged them in the correct order, spelling out the word *hope*. Brie smiled up at him.

"Hope," he confirmed. "Now you are worthy to dig for the treasure."

Brie looked at the map again and shook her head in confusion. There was no other secret spot on the map, just the four she had already discovered. She frowned for a moment, but then realized that Sir had drawn the two palm trees facing each other as well as the four torches.

There had to be a reason.

She glanced around the area, but saw nothing that drew her attention. She studied the placement of the four torches, assuming it must have some significance.

Brie looked back at the map, her brows furrowed. There was nothing to indicate where to start digging. She stared hard at Sir trying to figure out his thought process, and that's when she noticed he was standing in the middle of the four torches. A smile spread across her face.

"Sir, can I ask you to move?"

He nodded and stepped to the side. Brie laughed when she began to dig, thrilled to have succeeded in her task. Soon, however, she was sweating profusely but still hadn't found any treasure.

She stopped for a moment and looked at him. "Master?"

"Tenacity, téa."

That was enough encouragement to spur her on.

Brie went back to digging and was finally rewarded when she felt something hard. She eagerly dug around it until she could pull it out. With Sir's help, they brought up the old chest.

She instantly recognized it as the one they had uncovered in Italy.

She expected to find a bottle of wine inside. When Brie undid the clasp and opened the lid of the creaky chest, however, she didn't see anything. Leaning closer, she spied a tiny box hidden in the shadows of the chest. Picking it up, she smiled at Sir. "I almost don't want to open it, because then my treasure hunt will be over."

"Open it, Brie," he insisted.

The use of her given name let her know this was more than a game between Master and sub; this was a personal gift. She unlatched the miniature lock on the box and opened it. Inside was a tiny baby carriage made of silver. The wheels on it actually spun when she touched them. She looked up at Sir with tears in her eyes, unable to speak.

"You and our future child are my hope."

The tears began to flow down Brie's cheeks unchecked. He knelt beside her and held her in his strong embrace.

"What made you think to do this?" she asked, wiping at her tears.

Sir smiled warmly. "It was always my father's tradition to have a treasure hunt when we visited his island, and I wanted to continue that tradition with you—and our child."

Brie caressed his jaw, rough with stubble. "Thank you, Sir." She held up the tiny baby carriage in the firelight and smiled, no words necessary.

Sir kissed the top of her head. "Tonight we're simply Thane and Brie. A husband and wife enjoying the last day of their honeymoon together."

She lifted her chin to kiss him. "I love you, Thane Davis."

Saying his name still had the power to create butterflies in her stomach.

Confirmation

B rie set down her bags with a contented sigh. It felt so good to be back home!

Even though the honeymoon had been a whirlwind of romance and sexiness, there was something comforting about returning home. The feeling of belonging to a place had a powerful effect on her. It didn't hurt that it also smelled of the man she loved.

"Would you like me to unpack our things, Sir?"

He laughed. "No, I want you to undress and join me at the couch."

There were few things as wonderful and relaxing as kneeling at Sir's feet while he stroked her hair. She hurried off to the bedroom to relieve herself of her clothes.

She heard Sir make his way to the kitchen and soon the shaker sounded as he made them martinis. She made a quick stop in the bathroom to freshen up before returning to the living room.

Sir had undone his tie and unbuttoned his shirt, exposing his toned chest. "Kneel beside me and let me pet you, wife." It was the first time he'd called her that in the apartment and it made her all tingly inside.

On the surface, their lives had changed significantly since being away. Sir had been forced to let his mother die, and they had exchanged their wedding vows. Everything and nothing had changed—it was a paradox.

Brie rested her head on his thigh and purred in pleasure when he began running his fingers through her hair. "I love being home again."

"Travel has its thrills," he replied, "but home brings peace to the soul."

"I couldn't agree more, Sir."

He picked up his martini and took a long sip, sighing in satisfaction. Brie looked at the table and noticed he hadn't made one for her.

"Sir?" she asked, staring pointedly at his drink.

He reached over and took a small tumbler glass from the end table, handing it to her. Brie gratefully took a drink and then sputtered. "What the heck is this?"

"It's coconut water, my dear."

"Why?" she complained, setting it back on the table.

"Brie, you will be pregnant soon—if you aren't already."

She blushed at his assertion that she might already be pregnant, but she was *not* happy about the coconut water. "Why are you having me drink this poor substitute of a martini, Sir?"

"It's supposed to aid with your health and that of the baby's. Besides, we don't want the growth of our child to be influenced by alcohol at any stage of its development, especially early on."

She was touched that he cared, but thought it was silly for him to worry about it so soon. She asked him respectfully, "Don't you think you're being a little overprotective?"

He lifted her chin and looked directly into Brie's eyes to stress his point. "I want our child to be everything he or she is meant to be. Would you risk harming the baby while still in the womb?"

"Of course not..." she answered, looking down at the floor, suddenly feeling guilty and incredibly selfish.

Sir paused for a moment, then gently moved her before standing up. He collected both glasses and went back to the kitchen. She heard him using the shaker again, returning with two full martinis. He handed her the drink with a slight smirk.

Brie looked at him questioningly, surprised Sir had changed his mind after what he'd just shared. She stared at the glass warily, unsure if she should consume the alcohol knowing how concerned he was about it.

Was it a test?

"Drink," Sir commanded.

She took a small sip from the glass and broke out into a smile. "It's coconut water."

"As is mine. I will not ask you to do what I am unwilling to do myself."

Tears pricked her eyes. "You would do that for me?"

He held up his martini glass and answered, "For our child, Brie."

Brie clinked glasses with him. She gladly swallowed the lightly sweet water that hinted of the tropics. Knowing that they were in this together made all the difference to her.

She looked up at him shyly and asked in a bare whisper, "Do you really think I might be pregnant so soon?"

He smirked. "Wouldn't you say we've given it our best effort?"

She clinked his glass again. "We certainly have, Sir."

"I've held a suspicion that instant chemistry is actually an instinctual response—a subtle 'nudging' by Mother Nature that causes us to desire one person over another. I believe that most humans are attracted to those who are most likely to produce viable children based on compatible genetics. In fact, I'm convinced that's the reason your scent is so alluring to me and I feel the need to fuck you often."

"Genetics is not very romantic, Sir," Brie complained lightly.

"Romantic or not, wouldn't you agree it makes sense? If we use prehistoric man as an example, they copulated with those they were drawn to and continued the evolution of the human race by those couplings. It didn't matter whether their partner was their best friend or not."

"But that's not how it's done now," she answered defensively.

"No, we've decided to remain with one partner for life—not something that comes naturally for the human race."

She eyed him suspiciously. "Is that why you chose me, because you thought I was genetically compatible?"

Sir laughed. "No, Brie. If you recall, I never wanted to have children. It has nothing to do with genetics and everything to do with wanting to fuck you every day."

She couldn't help but smile at his answer.

He took a sip of his mock martini, winking at her. "I do believe you are already with child."

"Based solely on that argument?"

"No, I've noticed your temperature has changed."

She frowned, shaking her head. "Respectfully, Sir, how could you know my temperature has changed? Unless you've been secretly taking it at night when I'm asleep."

"Actually, babygirl, the last couple of days when we've been intimate, I've noticed a slight rise in your inner core temperature, and your nipples have become unusually sensitive. Both indicators of pregnancy."

She burned with a deeper blush, wondering if it were true.

"I didn't want to say anything in case I was wrong, but it has remained consistent enough to mention it now."

Brie put her hand to her lips, smiling to herself as her heart pounded at the thought. "Do you really think it's possible?"

"I do."

"But it's only been a few weeks…" she muttered.

"Of intense fucking."

She looked up at him and grinned.

"Why don't you drink the rest of the coconut water and take a pregnancy test? I stocked our bathroom with them in anticipation of this day."

Brie looked down at her lap, both excited and terrified at the prospect.

Oh wow…okay.

She downed the coconut water, still in shock at the idea of becoming a parent so quickly.

Brie left Sir to discover her fate. With shaking hands, she read the instructions before opening the box and unwrapping the testing stick. Taking a deep breath, she sat on the toilet and put it between her legs. She had used a plethora of BDSM tools in her young life, but this had to be the scariest instrument of all—it could prove potentially life-changing.

Naturally, the stress of the moment prevented her from being able to pee. After several minutes, Sir appeared at the door and asked with amusement, "Having problems?"

She looked up at him sheepishly. "I'm too nervous."

Sir turned on the sink faucet and smiled down at her. The sound of the running water had the desired effect, and she soon had the tester soaked. She laid the stick on the counter while she cleaned herself up. Sir stood behind her as they watched the blue line appear as it slowly traveled up the stick, indicating that the test was working.

Agonizing seconds ticked by as Brie watched the steady progress of the liquid while it continued to make its way up. Her heart almost stopped when the faint color of blue began to appear as a second line.

I'm pregnant…

"Hello, little mama." Sir said, wrapping his arms around her.

Brie closed her eyes, drinking in his protective embrace. When she opened them again, she gazed at Sir through the reflection of the mirror. Giggling nervously, she said, "Apparently you were right. We *are* a compatible couple."

Sir nodded, a confident smile on his lips. "No doubt my sperm enjoyed penetrating your egg."

Brie's heart skipped a beat thinking about that miraculous moment when their bodies had connected in the most intimate of ways—the creation of new life.

Sir turned her around to face him. "Are you okay, Brie? You're so quiet. You aren't having second thoughts, are you?"

She looked up at him, shaking her head as tears filled her eyes. "No, I just can't believe I'm having a baby. *Your* baby, Thane."

He leaned down and kissed her on the lips. Shivers coursed through her when he placed his hand on her flat stomach. "*Our* baby."

She covered his strong hand with her smaller ones, repeating, "Our baby." She smiled when she added, "We're going to be parents..."

Brie gazed into his eyes with concern. "How does it make you feel, Sir?"

He pursed his lips. "I won't lie, it's a sobering thought knowing there is another life I am soul-bound to protect."

Brie nodded. "It is daunting to have that kind of responsibility." She settled into his open arms and snuggled against his chest. "But how amazing to have our love actualized."

He kissed the top of her head. "That's a beautiful way to put it, babygirl."

"Are you happy, Thane?" Brie asked, not willing to look him in the eye when she said it.

He lifted her chin, his eyes shining brightly. "I am content, and that says a lot coming from me." He kissed her gently. "Happiness is a fleeting state I do not trust. However, contentment is an underlying emotion that cannot be easily influenced. To feel content in this moment confirms our choice to begin a family now."

She remained in his embrace as she stared at the two lines that marked the next season of her life. What did the future have in store for her—for them?

"So whom do we call first?" Sir asked her, interrupting her wandering thoughts.

"My parents and your aunt and uncle. Our families will be so excited!"

Sir stroked his chin thoughtfully. "I suppose Durov should be informed as well."

Brie giggled excitedly, "I can't even begin to imagine how crazy this news will make him."

"Hmm… That gives me food for thought," he stated, his eyes twinkling impishly. "I believe that Brad should be told in person," Sir stated, laughing to himself. "I cannot wait to see his reaction."

Brie grimaced. "Master Anderson really doesn't like children."

"Which should make telling him quite entertaining."

Naturally, Brie's mother responded as a mother

should—with a loud, enthusiastic scream before she shouted into the phone, "We're going to be grandparents!"

Her father was less enthusiastic. "So soon, Brie?"

She could only giggle at his lackluster response. "Yes, Daddy. You're going to be a grandpa in nine months. Can you believe it?"

"No, daughter, I cannot."

"But admit it, you're excited about being a grandpa. What are you planning to have the baby call you? Is it going to be Gampa, Granpoppy, or maybe Pawpee?"

Even though he tried to mask it, she heard the elation in his voice when he answered, "Much too soon to be thinking about those things, young lady."

"Well, be sure to let me know so I can start referring to you properly when I talk to my tummy."

Sir called Mr. Reynolds next, who was left speechless when he heard the news.

"Mr. Reynolds?"

"Unc?" Sir asked in concern when the silence continued.

"I'm sorry, you two. I'm just feeling a bit overwhelmed right now. Thane, when I think where you have been and where you are now, I couldn't feel more…proud."

Tears formed in Sir's eyes. "I have appreciated your support all these years, Unc. Even in the beginning when I didn't show it."

"I understood, Thane, believe me. I always trusted you would overcome the sins of my sister. But to see your life now, it's… it is far better than anything I'd ever hoped for. You are a truly remarkable man."

"No," Sir answered. "I'm simply a survivor who was lucky enough to meet your little tobacco shop girl."

Mr. Reynolds laughed. "Never would have guessed my star employee would end up being the mother of your child." He added teasingly, "I've never quite forgiven you for stealing my best employee."

Brie giggled. "As much as I enjoyed working for you, Unc, I much prefer my life now."

"No doubt, young lady," he said with a kind chuckle, "but Thane owes me, wouldn't you agree?"

Judy jumped into the conversation, "Honey, expect a package to be coming soon. I want to send you and Thane a little surprise to celebrate your happy news."

It warmed Brie's heart that Judy was excited about the baby. The Reynolds acted as wonderful replacements for the parents Sir lost. Ever since that fateful day when Mr. Reynolds' sister Ruth had ruined Sir's life, he'd done nothing but show love, patience and support to his nephew.

"Thank you, Judy," Sir replied. "And Unc, I do agree I owe you something for bringing Brie and I together."

Mr. Reynolds laughed uncomfortably. "No, no, Thane. I was only jesting. I had nothing to do with it. You were the one who found her, but she was the one who claimed you."

Sir gave Brie a sideways glance. "Interesting way to put it…"

"I knew Brie was something special the moment I interviewed her for the job. Little did I know the impact she would have on my life and yours. The best part for me is that I'm now going to be a grandpa. Judy and I could never have kids, but through you two, we'll get to know the joy of being grandparents. What an incredible gift…one I never thought would happen for us."

"We are just so happy!" Judy cried into the phone.

"We are too!" Brie shouted back.

After that entertaining phone call, Brie went to dial Rytsar's number next.

"No, Brie. I have something else in mind for my Russian brother."

Brie laughed. "What are you planning, Sir?"

"He deserves a special announcement, wouldn't you agree?"

"Sure…"

"I'm not a sadist, so there is no need to worry. Cruel jokes aren't my forte. While I get the needed item, I'll need you to find a graphic of a circle with a red diagonal line through it."

Brie googled images after he left until she found a clear one without any other text. It didn't take Sir long to return with a bottle of Zyr vodka from the corner liquor store.

"Oh, I see where you are headed with this," she said approvingly.

Per Sir's instructions, Brie printed and cut out the image. Sir took it from her and used clear packing tape to secure it. "Think that's obvious enough?" he asked, holding up the bottle.

"I think he will love it."

Sir took a picture and sent it to Rytsar. "It's almost three a.m. there—think he'll respond?"

Before Brie could answer, Sir's phone rang and Brie heard Rytsar clearly shout, "I'm a dyadya!"

Sir laughed as he put his friend on speaker phone. "It's true, old friend."

"So you finally made your fucking count, *moy droog,*" he complimented.

"Need I remind you that we just got back from the honeymoon?" Sir replied dryly.

"*Radost moya* would have been pregnant the day of the wedding if it had been me."

Sir rolled his eyes, making Brie giggle.

"How are you feeling, *radost moya*? Are you sick? Do you need to come here so I can tend you?"

"I'm feeling wonderful, Rytsar, thank you."

"So is it a boy or a girl?"

She giggled. "We don't know that yet. The baby's still just a zygote."

"A zy-what?"

"A bunch of cells. It can't even be called an embryo yet."

"You and your scientific words," he scoffed. "You're pregnant with *moye solntse.*"

"What's *moye solntse*? It sounds so beautiful when you say it."

"It's her name, *radost moya,*" he insisted without further explanation.

Brie turned to Sir and whispered, "What does it mean?"

"My sunshine."

"Oh…" Tears came to Brie's eyes. "I love that name, Rytsar."

Sir stated sarcastically, "You do realize we may have a boy, old friend."

Rytsar only laughed.

But Brie was suddenly concerned. "You will still love our baby if it's a boy…won't you?"

"I will love your child," Rytsar assured her.

Brie let out a sigh of relief. "Good, because you're going to make a wonderful uncle."

"*Dyadya*," he corrected.

"Of course," she said with a grin. "*Dyadya* forever and always."

"Who else has been told, comrade?"

"Just Brie's parents and my Unc." Sir paused for a moment. "Oh, and Nosaka."

The line went silent.

Sir winked at Brie.

"What?" Rytsar roared, upset by the answer.

Sir started to chuckle. "You're too easy, old friend."

"Oh, so you jest?"

Brie laughed out loud. "Sorry, Rytsar, but that was funny."

"Fine, you two can have your laugh at my expense as long as I am named the godfather."

"We're not striking deals here," Sir scoffed.

"It is only right as your brother."

Brie could hear the serious tone in Rytsar's voice and touched Sir's arm in warning.

Sir nodded, hearing it too. "We will discuss those things at a later date. Right now you need to go back to sleep and we have other calls to make."

"*Radost moya*, take care of yourself and the babe."

"I will, Rytsar."

"Frankly, I do not know how I will go back to sleep after this, but goodnight, *moy droog*. You have made me a happy man."

Sir put his arm around Brie. "That makes two of us."

Brie wanted to call Lea and Mary next, telling them at the same time via video chat. Unfortunately, Lea wasn't answering her phone, and Brie didn't want her to miss the big news, so she left a message to call back as soon as possible.

"Who next, Sir?"

"I think we need to invite Brad over for dinner. Don't you?"

She shook her head, amused at the idea of telling him over a meal. "We are not very nice people, you and I. So what day?"

"Why wait? Let's meet him someplace tonight. I don't think either of us want to cook."

"Very true," Brie agreed. Last thing she needed was the challenge of coming up with something edible when their fridge had been empty for more than two weeks. She giggled evilly when she hit dial.

Master Anderson had only gotten into LA a short time before they returned home from their honeymoon, so Brie was sure he had a houseful of boxes he was still sifting through. Going out for dinner might be exactly what he needed.

"Hello, Master Anderson?"

"Is that you, young Brie? Back from the honeymoon so soon?"

"Yep, our fantasy vacation is over and the daily grind

begins."

"Where did you guys end up going?"

"Actually, Sir and I wanted to tell you about it in person. Care to join us for dinner?"

"Hell yeah! I am so sick of living out of boxes. Let me meet you at that sports bar close to you guys. I gotta get far away from this mess until I get some order here."

Brie thought it was the perfect choice, considering neither she nor Sir would be ordering drinks. "See you in an hour?"

"Make it forty-five minutes. I seriously need the distraction."

Oh, you'll be distracted all right, she thought. Out loud she told him, "We'll see you then."

Master Anderson was already waiting for them when they entered the noisy bar. He gestured them over and asked enthusiastically, "What'll you have? I'm buying the first round for the married couple."

Brie looked at Sir before ordering. "I would love an iced tea."

"One Long Island coming up," he announced, looking to Sir.

"Actually, just a plain old tea. My tummy has been acting up," Brie explained.

Master Anderson frowned. "Sorry to hear that. Must have been all those foreign places you visited. It can be hard on a body adjusting to unfamiliar foods."

He turned to Sir, grasping his shoulder in a friendly manner. "What about you, my friend? Martini, shot of vodka or whiskey?"

Sir thought about it before he answered. "A glass of milk would suffice."

Master Anderson's jaw dropped. "Milk?"

Sir shrugged. "A secret pleasure of mine."

"Seriously? Is your stomach acting up, too?"

"You could say that."

Master Anderson shook his head in disgust as he ordered their drinks, adding a tall beer and a shot of whiskey straight up for himself. "Remind me never to get married or, at the very least, never to go to a foreign country for the honeymoon." He looked at Sir seriously. "Did you spend your entire honeymoon hovering over the toilet, man?"

"Rest assured, this is a recent condition."

"Well, that's a relief!" He winked at Brie. "Would hate to think of you playing nursemaid for your husband on your honeymoon."

"Oh, we had such a wonderful time, Master Anderson!" Brie gushed. "From Venice to Fiji, all of it was a dream come true for me."

"Fiji, huh?" He glanced at Sir. "What does Fiji have that America doesn't?"

"Privacy," Sir stated simply, taking the glass of milk the waitress offered him. He smiled as he put the white substance to his lips.

"Nope, I'm not going to do it." Master Anderson turned his attention on Brie, bringing his hand up to shield his eyes from Sir. "I cannot watch him drink that stuff."

Brie giggled as she squeezed the slice of lemon from the rim of her glass into her iced tea and stirred it. "So Master Anderson, are you almost moved in?"

"Far from it."

"Oh, do you want some help?"

Sir frowned. "Brie, I don't think you should."

Master Anderson looked at him strangely. "Shouldn't what? You know you can trust me with her."

"It's not that."

"What then?" He let out a huff of exasperation. "What's wrong with the man?" he demanded of Brie. "Did he get kidnapped by aliens on your trip?"

Brie smiled, but addressed Sir. "I'm sure I'll be fine. Really, you don't have to be so protective."

Master Anderson punched Sir on the shoulder. "That's right, Thane, just because you're married now doesn't mean young Brie isn't perfectly capable of taking care of herself."

"She's not the only one I'm looking out for."

Master Anderson crinkled his brow. "What are you talking about? Are you high on something? Hell, maybe I am and I just don't know it—because none of this is making sense to me."

Brie put her hand over Sir's, batting her eyes at her Master. "I appreciate that you feel so protective about us."

Master Anderson turned his head sharply toward her. "Did you just say *us?*"

Brie smiled sweetly when she answered. "I did, Master Anderson."

He looked back at Sir, staring hard at his friend. "Uh uh...there's no way." His expression changed to one of mirth as he threw his head back and laughed. "Oh man, you had me going there for a moment."

"I fail to see what's so funny," Sir stated calmly.

Master Anderson punched his shoulder again. "Okay, okay, you've had your fun. Let me order you a real drink. Heck, I'll make it two because you got me so good."

Sir smiled. "You could order the drinks, but I would still not be able to drink them."

"Why the hell not?"

"I have made a promise to Brie."

Master Anderson eyed him suspiciously. "What kind of promise, Thane?"

"Not to drink any alcohol until she can."

Master Anderson turned back to Brie. "He's kidding right? Just can't let the joke die."

Brie broke into a huge smile. "Master Anderson, it's true. I'm pregnant."

He stared at her for several uncomfortable moments as if it hadn't registered. He glanced at Sir before saying, "Oh, young Brie..." Taking her small hand and holding it tenderly between his, Master Anderson added in a solemn tone, "I'm so sorry."

Brie burst into giggles. "There's nothing to be sorry about. I'm very happy, aren't you?"

He pulled his hands away from her, shaking his head. "I wish I could tell you yes, but it would be a lie. If what you say is true, Thane just threw your life away with that irresponsible cock of his."

Sir raised an eyebrow. "You know, if you weren't my friend I might deck you right now."

"Hey buddy, I'm not the idiot who forgot to wear a condom on his honeymoon."

Brie tsked. "He did no such thing. We wanted to have a baby. How could we know we'd be incredibly compatible?"

Master Anderson stared at Sir in utter shock. "*You* wanted this?"

Sir nodded. "After careful consideration and much soul searching I decided this was the best course for us as a couple."

"You?" Master Anderson shook his head as if trying to clear it. "Thane, I can't believe it. I have known you for a long, long time. Kids are not something you do. They're not something either of us do. Am I right?"

Sir answered in an unruffled tone, "Yes, that was true—until now."

"What the hell changed, bud?" Master Anderson asked with complete sincerity.

"L.B.B., my friend."

"What?"

Sir took Brie's hand and kissed the top of it. "I have a new life now."

Master Anderson threw his arms in the air. "Oh, I can just see it now… Brie with one kid hanging off her hip and another attached to her boob, while you sit back in your rocking chair drinking a beer."

Sir only smirked.

"Brie, is this really what you want?" Master Anderson asked. "You deserve more than a vanilla life, young lady."

Her eyes sparkled in amusement when she answered, rubbing her tummy for emphasis. "I want a family. I couldn't be happier than I am right now."

Seeing he wasn't getting anywhere with her, Master Anderson focused back on Sir. "Buddy, what were you thinking? Do you really plan on bringing a screaming, snot-nosed kid to the Haven—seriously? 'Cause people aren't going to take kindly to that shit."

Sir chuckled. "You do realize there are such things as babysitters."

Master Anderson shook his finger at Sir. "I know how this goes down. You'll cart that thing everywhere and expect the rest of us to tell you how cute it is, even when it…" he crinkled his nose in mock disgust. "—smells."

Sir laughed out loud. "I *am* capable of changing diapers."

Master Anderson ignored his statement, looking at Brie sadly. "This will be the end of you, young lady." He gave Sir the same sorrowful look. "It was nice knowing you, Thane. You were a good friend to me."

"I'm not dying," Sir admonished.

Master Anderson shook his head. "You might as well be, buddy…you might as well be." He downed his beer in several long, deep gulps.

Sir got an evil twinkle in his eye when he told Master Anderson, "By the way, I was only kidding."

"Thank God!" Master Anderson shouted in relief, so loudly that the other patrons turned towards them wanting to know what had him so happy. He stood up and announced to the whole bar, "My friend is *not* having a baby!"

Master Anderson sat back down, looking like his old self again.

"I was kidding about liking milk." Sir said, pushing the glass away from him as he graced Master Anderson with a wicked smile. "I can't stand the stuff."

"Oh hell," Master Anderson cried. "Thane, you're seriously messing with my head."

Brie responded to his genuine distress by getting up from her chair and giving Master Anderson a hug. "You're going to be an honorary uncle to our child, that's the honest truth."

He patted her arm. "Well…I guess I can live with that."

She gave him a chaste kiss on the cheek before whispering in his ear, "And you're not allowed to ever call him or her an *it* again."

Master Anderson chuckled under his breath. "Deal."

Tantra Treat

I t wasn't until the next day that Brie was able to video chat with both Lea and Mary. She knew Mary would give her crap about getting pregnant, but Brie was curious how Lea would react—plus she was dying to know what had happened with Rytsar in Italy.

"Hey, you two!" Brie squealed when she saw Lea's smiling face and Mary's sarcastic expression on her tablet.

"What's up, girlfriend?" Lea cried.

Mary said with a listless tone, "Hey, Brie the Married."

"Girls, you will NEVER guess my big news!"

"Oh wait…oh wait, you're divorced," Mary answered. "Way to go, loser."

Lea ignored Mary, squinting at Brie as if she were looking for something. "Is that a rosy blush I see?"

"Maybe," Brie answered.

"No freakin' way. You're preggers!"

"WTF?" Mary exclaimed.

Brie smiled as she vigorously nodded her confirmation.

"Why would you let this happen?" Mary asked in shock.

Mary's reaction was similar to Master Anderson's, and it made Brie smile. "We didn't *let* it happen, we caused it to happen."

"But why? Your life is over now."

"Stop being a sour puss, Mary," Lea scolded. "This is happy news!"

"It is happy news," Brie agreed joyfully. "I've been flying on cloud nine ever since we found out."

"So you puking yet?" Mary wanted to know.

"Nope, I don't feel any different."

Mary gave her a disbelieving look. "Then how could you possibly know?"

"It was Sir, actually. He said he noticed a change in my temperature and insisted I take the test when we got back."

"So you're really JUST pregnant, like it just happened?" Lea squeaked.

Brie grinned. "Sir has some very active sperm."

Lea's eyes lit up. "Hey, what do sperm and lawyers have in common?"

"Don't do it, Lea," Mary warned.

Brie couldn't help herself, giggling when she asked, "I don't know, what do sperm and lawyers have in common?"

"Only one in a million have a chance of becoming a human being."

Mary groaned while Brie covered her mouth, trying to choke down her laughter unsuccessfully.

"Oh yeah, you liked that one."

Brie erupted in giggles.

"Those hormones *must* be messing with Brie," Mary complained, "because she actually thought that was funny."

"You know what would be funnier?" Lea chortled. "If I changed the joke from lawyers to pharmacists."

"Are you trying to pick a fight, big boobs?"

Brie couldn't stop laughing. "I've missed you two bickering."

Lea ignored Mary, her eyes sparkling with interest. "So I have to assume the honeymoon was AMAZING!"

"Yep, even better than the wedding."

"So where did you guys go?"

"We had *the* most romantic experience in Venice with a kinky group of Italians and then…" she paused for dramatic effect, "Sir took me to a private island in Fiji."

"And the island is where you got pregnant," Mary surmised.

"I'm not so sure. You see, Sir reserved a honeymoon suite in Venice famous for blessing newlyweds with pregnancy."

"Oooh…" Lea cooed. "Did it have all kinds of fertility aids?"

Brie shook her head. "No, it was a regular room, but I tell ya, Lea, there was something magical about that room. Best sex ever! I hated to leave it."

"Hmm…maybe I should look into that room," Lea mused. "Of course, I would make sure the guy wore triple condoms."

"Wise. I have to say while Venice was romantically hot, but the island was primal and wicked."

"Was it an exclusive resort?"

"No. I was expecting that too, Lea, but Sir found a deserted island where someone had built the cutest miniature house. We were castaways on that tiny island for a whole week."

"Sand sex sucks," Mary interjected.

Brie grinned, nodding. "Yes, it does, but Sir prepared for that. We had a shower in the tiny house, so we had no sand in unwanted places."

"So basically," Mary said with a smirk, "Fiji was a week of banging like rabbits?"

"Naturally, there was a lot of sex," Brie snorted. "However, Sir brought a bag of tools and treated me to a week of fantasies—both his and mine."

"Damn, girlfriend, that sounds so yummy!" Lea purred.

"It was. It truly was…" Brie answered in a wistful voice, remembering their many encounters.

"Now that we have the low-down on where and how you got laid," Mary stated, "I want to know what happened with Rytsar, Lea the Lame."

Lea's eyes widened, her mouth clamping shut tight.

Her friend's reaction surprised Brie.

Avoiding the question altogether, Lea smiled and asked Brie, "So what's it like knowing you're pregnant?"

Brie graciously accepted the change of subject, determined to ask her about Rytsar later, and answered, "It's kind of crazy and wonderful." She felt a warm feeling just thinking about having Thane's baby.

Lea asked gently, "Are you ready to become a mother?"

Brie's smile faltered a little. "To be honest, I'm a bit scared. I mean, what do I know about caring for a baby? What if I suck at it?"

Mary almost said something, but bit back her comment. "That one was too easy."

Brie gave her a knowing wink.

Lea seemed genuine when she offered, "I don't know anything about babies either, but if you need me I'll come." Then she quickly added, "Just don't make me change a diaper or burp the baby. I can't stand spit up." She gagged a little to prove her point.

"Lea, since that's all parents do those first few months, you'd be totally useless to Brie," Mary stated.

"Not completely useless," Lea replied, "because I know exactly what to do when a baby cries. I can totally handle it like a professional."

Brie looked at her skeptically. "Really?"

"Oh, totally," she answered with confidence.

"So what do you do?" Brie asked, hoping Lea held some secret passed down in her family.

"I hand them back to their mothers. Easy peasy."

Brie couldn't believe she'd fallen for Lea's tease and started laughing again.

"You fell right into that one," Mary grumbled. "Really Brie, I think those hormones have stolen your brain or something."

Brie rolled her eyes, having way too much fun with the girls, but there was a serious question still to ask. She attempted to approach it nonchalantly. "So Lea, are you coming back to LA?"

Lea looked at her sadly. "I know you aren't going to like this, but I don't think I can any time soon."

"Why not?"

"With all the changes going on at the Denver Academy since Master Anderson's exit, Mistress Clark seriously needs my assistance."

"Did she ask for it?"

"No," Lea answered defensively, "but I see how hard she's working, struggling to keep the Academy running smoothly on her own."

"Lea…"

"Leave her alone, Brie. Lea's a big girl and can do what she wants. The real question is does Ms. Clark know about you and Rytsar?"

"Hell no!" Lea blurted.

"I want to know what happened with the Russian. Spill, big boobs."

"I always knew you were jealous of my girls, Mary," Lea joked, pushing up her breasts and wiggling them enticingly. However, she took the bait and confessed, "I've been dying to tell someone about Rytsar."

"Talk at your own risk," Brie cautioned.

Lea shrugged. "You know I can't keep anything to myself, but Mary, you have to promise, cross-your-heart-and-hope-to-die, that you won't tell Mistress Clark what I'm about to share."

Mary snorted. "I haven't said anything yet, have I?"

"Cross your heart," Lea insisted.

Mary rolled her eyes as she made a cross over her heart. "Happy now?"

Lea giggled. "I just wanted to see you do that." She pushed her boobs up one more time for Mary's benefit before beginning. "As you know, I took up Rytsar up on his offer after breakfast."

"Yeah, we both saw it," Brie remarked. "Shocked the heck out of me at the time."

Lea's grin grew wider. "Well…I must say I totally understand why you and Mistress Clark had the hots for the sexy Russian."

"How is he any different than any other Dom?" Mary demanded.

Lea laughed like a giddy child, shaking her head. "Oh, that man…"

Brie smiled dreamily, knowing exactly what she meant. "Truly one of a kind."

"What's so great about him?" Mary insisted.

Lea just grinned, staring off into space as if lost in a memory. Finally, she replied, "Rytsar showed me things I never knew…"

"Did he use his cat o' nines?" Brie asked her. When Lea shivered, Brie had her answer. "Did he really do it in the dungeon?"

Lea only nodded, a blush creeping up her impressive chest.

"Oh wow, based on that blush, girl, you must have been much braver than me."

"Stop leaving me out of this conversation," Mary huffed irritably.

"Sorry, Mary—unless you've scened with Rytsar, you can't understand the power of the man," Lea explained. "Hell, I didn't get it until I was under his dominance."

Lea fanned herself. "So freakin' H-O-T…"

Mary got a smug look on her face. "You must have felt downright wicked, knowing how Ms. Clark pined for years over that Russian."

Lea's blush rose up to her cheeks.

"I have to say, I was totally surprise when you agreed to his invitation, Lea," Brie confessed.

"I'll admit I might have been suffering a moment of spitefulness. Heck, it gets tiresome being constantly rejected by the woman you love, but…" She burst into a huge grin. "I'm so glad I did!"

"You're going to hell for this, big boobs, but for the first time I actually respect you."

Lea waved off Mary's comment. "You're just jealous. Nah, nah."

Brie giggled again, thrilled to see Lea so happy. "So you actually like Rytsar's brand of kink?"

Lea bit her lip playfully, getting that far-off look again. "I experienced a lot that night, and his aftercare was so divine…" She looked at Brie mischievously. "I even have marks."

Mary pouted. "Why didn't I ever play with him? Damn it!"

"Definitely your loss, woman," Lea replied, smirking at her.

"So, do you think you'll ever scene with Rytsar again?" Brie asked.

The shade of her blush turned a bright lobster red. Brie couldn't begin to guess what that meant but didn't want to dive any deeper at the moment. She turned the conversation to Mary, who seemed frustrated. "So how's the collared life treating you these days?"

Mary sat up a little straighter as she fingered the metal collar around her neck. "I'm still getting used to it."

"What do you mean?" Lea asked, eager to have the heat off her.

"It's a struggle sometimes, knowing I'm not free. It's harder than I thought it would be."

"Isn't Faelan pretty open to you playing with others?" Brie asked, remembering how he'd been at the Sanctuary in Montana.

"Yeah…" Mary answered, pausing for a moment. "But I feel caged. I can't explain why. God knows I *want* to be happy with Faelan."

"Have you told Faelan this?" Brie pressed, now concerned not only for Mary, but Faelan's heart.

"Of course not! It would only hurt him. You know how much he's been through already. But I can't shake this feeling."

Brie felt a sense of foreboding but advised, "It's natural to have an adjustment period. Sir and I certainly did. It's completely normal."

"I hear you, Stinky Cheese, but let me put it to you this way. When I hear Lea go on and on about the Russian, I can't help but feel I'm missing out big time. I don't think I'm cut out to be collared to one man."

Brie looked at her sympathetically. "Mary, do you remember how desperate you felt when you lost Faelan? Even when you were at the Sanctuary with all those men, you said it meant nothing without him."

Pain flitted across her eyes. "I do remember…" Her voice quavered when she admitted, "I don't know what's wrong with me, Brie. When I don't have Faelan, I'm miserable. When I'm with him, I feel the need to break free again."

"Faelan loves you, Mary. You couldn't ask for a better-suited Dom," Lea assured her.

"I know that. Don't you think I know that? That's why this hurts so much…"

"It's easy to feel the grass is greener on the other side, but it's unhealthy to think that way when you're in a committed relationship," Brie told her.

Mary's hard exterior crumbled briefly, her voice breaking when she confessed, "I hate the thought of hurting him."

"Please, Mary, don't," Brie begged. "Tell him how you're feeling. Give him a chance to deal with the doubts you're experiencing."

"I don't think you understand, Brie. The day I tell him is the day I walk away."

Brie closed her eyes, already feeling Faelan's pain. "Promise me you'll give yourself time to work through these feelings. Commitments this deep take time."

"How long, Brie?" Mary asked. "How long do I wait when everything in me is telling me to run?"

Lea's eyes lit up. "Have you thought of talking to Captain?"

"No," Mary snapped. "I don't want Vader involved in this."

But Brie agreed with Lea, thinking it was a brilliant suggestion. "Captain is perfect because he knows the situation and respects you."

Mary suddenly took on the look of the Blonde Nemesis of old when she hissed, "Don't you *dare* fucking tell him!"

Brie shot back angrily, "Don't worry about me. He would expect to hear from you if you're having trouble. Talking to Captain is on your shoulders, not mine."

"I don't get you, Mary," Lea complained. "Not one little iota."

"Women are so stupid," Mary growled. "I don't even know why I bother telling you two anything."

"Because you know we're bound together for life—a gift from the Submissive Training Center," Brie affirmed. She didn't want Mary doing something rash, something she would regret forever so Brie reminded her, "I'm here if you need me, day or night. That hasn't changed."

"Even though you irritate the crap out of me, the same goes for me, Stinky Cheese." Mary paused for a moment and added, "Even you, big boobs."

"Aren't you just a big old softie under those razor sharp claws?" Lea cooed.

Brie laughed nervously, hoping their friendship would be enough to see Mary through. It seemed whenever things were going well for Mary, she felt compelled to ruin it.

"So Brie, you haven't brought it up… I gotta ask. How much money did get for your wedding?" A curl of a smile showed up on Mary's red lips.

Brie blushed and said nothing.

"That wasn't rude to ask, was it?"

"Not at all, Mary. I'm curious too," Lea answered, smiling at Brie.

"Sorry, you guys. I hate to admit this, but I haven't

opened them yet. In fact, I totally forgot until you mentioned it just now."

"Well, you better get to it, woman. Inquiring minds want to know."

Lea broke out in giggles. "Subbie time is always a hoot. I just love us!"

"Me too!" Brie agreed.

Both girls stared at Mary expectantly. She finally rolled her eyes, added in a lackluster voice, "Me three."

Lea declared joyfully, her breasts jiggling as she bounced on her seat, "The Three Musketeers of Submission rise again! Oh my gosh, this calls for another joke!" She grinned, "What did one ovary say to the other ovary?"

"No clue," Brie encouraged.

"If that dick comes in here again, let's throw eggs at him!"

Mary gave her a death stare that made Brie burst out in giggles.

"Another point for me!" Lea announced, kissing her finger and making a sizzling sound as she touched her butt.

The video chat ended with multiple groans. Brie looked out the bedroom window as she undressed and lay her clothes in the top drawer of the dresser. She worried about Lea not coming to LA and what that might mean for her friend. She was also deeply concerned about Mary and Faelan.

She had to laugh at herself. "Heck, it's like I'm a mother already the way I worry about everyone. Having this baby should be easy peasy."

Brie sought Sir out, needing his physical strength to calm the concerns whirling in her heart.

"Sir, may I kneel at your feet?"

"Certainly," he said, gesturing her to come to him.

Brie sighed in contentment when her cheek lay against his muscular thigh. That simple contact was enough, but when he began stroking her hair the tingling started and erased all other thought.

It was just her and her Master—nothing else mattered.

"Is anything wrong?" he asked after several minutes.

She kept her gaze directed at the cityscape outside the window. "I don't know how to help my friends, Sir." She knew Sir did not like gossip so only told him, "Lea's not coming to LA, and Mary is having her own struggles."

Sir sighed heavily. "There comes a point when all we can do is sit back and allow things to play out the way they must. I struggled with Durov and Samantha's situation back in college. It gutted me that it fell apart so violently, but I quickly came to realize it was not my place to interfere. My role was to help both survive the aftermath so they could eventually move on from it with the friendship I had with each still intact."

"Speaking of Rytsar, Sir, you might be interested to know Lea spent time with him after we left for our honeymoon."

"Did they scene together?" Sir asked firmly.

Brie hesitated to answer him but gave a simple, "Yes."

"Damn," Sir groaned. "Durov couldn't have been

aware of the history between Lea and Samantha. He would never have entangled himself with her if he'd known."

"They hooked up at the breakfast, Sir. I didn't stop them when they left together because I wasn't sure how to react."

Sir resumed stroking her hair after considering the unwanted revelation. "I wished I'd noticed, if only to warn him of Lea's history with Samantha." He sighed again in frustration. "Well, there's nothing to be done now but watch it play out. I will, however, give Durov a heads-up so he's not blindsided should something come of this."

"Lea isn't planning to tell Ms. Clark," Brie assured him.

"The truth always comes out."

She looked up at him and confessed, "I can't help worrying about my friends because I don't want any of them to get hurt."

He cradled her chin. "That is a part of life, and not something you can prevent." Sir moved, opening his legs. "Right now I want you to live in the moment. Sit right here," he directed, indicating the spot between his legs, "and face the window."

Brie smiled as she sat between his muscular thighs, liking the feeling of their strength pressed against her body.

"I want you to close your eyes."

She did and soon felt pleasant chills as Sir lifted her hair and lightly kissed the side of her neck. He twisted her hair tighter, moving to the other side.

"Oh, Sir…"

He gently pushed her head forward and kissed the nape of her neck. A current of electricity traveled down, warming not only her heart. His tender kisses expressed his love, but also helped to heighten her desire for him.

"See what you do to me?" he whispered in her ear, taking her hand and moving it behind her to feel the hardness of his cock. Sir grabbed onto her waist and pushed her ass against it for emphasis. "Even though we have succeeded in our quest to get you pregnant, I'm feeling the insatiable need to fuck you again. It hasn't dissipated."

"I feel the same way, Sir."

She gasped when he tightened his grip on her hair, pulling it to the side to lightly bite her neck. The sensation increased her arousal ten-fold.

"Do you see that tantra chair over there?" he asked in a husky voice.

"I do," she affirmed lustfully.

"Go to it and lay in the position you want me to take you."

Brie was excited by an impromptu session and stood up, sauntering over to it with the grace of a cat. She lay down, cradled in its comfortable curvature, and smiled up at him.

"Face to face again?"

"Please, Sir." She didn't explain why she had requested the position, wanting to surprise him.

Sir shook his head, a smirk on his face. He stripped in front of her, throwing his clothes on the couch haphazardly. Standing over her, his cock announced itself, stiff with need.

"Open your legs to me," he commanded.

Brie positioned them on either side of the tantra chair, leaving her sex fully exposed to him. He looked down at her with hunger in his eyes. "Your pussy is already pink and slippery with desire."

"Your touch has that effect on me."

He lowered himself onto her, sliding his cock into her opening without resistance. Resting both hands above her head for better control, he rolled his hips, giving her the full depth of his love. Brie watched in rapt adoration as his muscles tensed and released with each controlled stroke.

"You're sexy to watch when you make love to me," she admitted, a playful smile on her lips.

"As are you, wife." He reached down, playing with a breast as he continued to stroke her with his shaft. She tilted her pelvis, seeking even more depth from him.

"Greedy little thing, aren't you?" Sir stopped for a moment, gazing into her eyes. "I love that ravenous need in you."

"Only for you," she whispered.

Sir met her insatiable need, increasing the depth but not the pace, keeping it a slow, controlled thrust as he looked down at her. The expression on his face was as tender as it was lustful.

Brie licked her lips provocatively. "May I eat you, Sir?"

"Now?"

"Yes, I want to take your cock into my mouth and suck until you come."

He immediately pulled out, closing his eyes as his cock pulsed on her stomach. "You test me, woman."

"Only because I love your cock so very much."

"One second," he announced, abandoning her on the tantra chair to walk back to their bedroom. A minute later, he returned with the Magic Wand in his hand.

Brie eyes widened as he plugged it in and switched the toy on.

"You can eat me as long as I get to play with your pussy using this."

Brie nodded, excited by the prospect.

Sir straddled her, lowering himself so his cock was level with her lips. She opened her mouth and guided him in with her hand as he reached behind and settled the buzzing toy on her clit. Her pelvis jumped of its own accord, reacting to the vigorous vibration. Sir tasted of pre-come mixed with her own excitement, the combination an exhilarating treat for her senses.

"Stay still," he commanded.

Brie moaned her agreement on his shaft, closing her eyes to concentrate on the seductive in and out motion of his cock as she took it deeper down her throat.

The buzz of the wand had her pussy climbing quickly to orgasm. She momentarily broke the embrace of her lips to ask, "May I come, Sir?"

"So soon?"

"Eating you and feeling that wand is too sexy to handle."

He smirked. "I'm feeling generous. By all means, take me back in your mouth and come."

Brie smiled as she opened her mouth to invite him

in, thrilled that he was allowing her the freedom to orgasm.

Her nipples hardened as he began fucking her mouth slowly while the Magic Wand buzzed so alluringly on her mound. The dual sensation of sucking his shaft while her pussy was vigorously stimulated by the toy reminded her of their threesomes with Rytsar. It didn't take long for the climax to peak, but it was so strong her whole body shuddered when she came.

"Holy hell, do that again," he panted, looking down at her amorously.

Brie looked up at him, sucking harder as he grasped her neck possessively with his other hand, stating his dominance physically and making her submission to him complete.

Another hard orgasm wracked her body, and she groaned from the intensity of it.

Sir pulled out, his eyes burning with desire. "That one almost broke my resolve."

"Please come, Sir…I long…to taste you," she replied in gasps.

"I will fulfill that need only because it pleases me to do so."

She smiled, grateful he was being so agreeable.

He turned off the wand and put it down for a moment, running his fingers over her trembling pussy. "So wet. I bet that tastes sweet. Shall we make it even sweeter?"

"Please, Sir," she purred.

He turned the toy back on, but at the higher level and said with a wicked grin, "I won't be gentle."

"I don't want you to be."

He held her head still and commanded her to suck. Brie licked her lips in anticipation just before she took his hard shaft. Sir placed the wand on her clit at the perfect angle and she cried out, her whole body humming.

Sir began to pump her mouth as the wand had its way with her pussy. He put his hand around her neck again, growling low.

Holy. Freaking. Hell.

She started whimpering in pleasure, her muscles tensing for a massive come. Her body stilled just before it hit. In response, Sir pushed himself deeper and held himself there.

Her orgasm was so intense, Brie became a slave to it—her body jerking forcefully as water gushed from deep inside, covering her thighs and the wand with her juices.

She heard Sir's intake of breath as his cock began pulsing in her throat as he orgasmed.

It was heavenly, decadent, and so incredibly sexy for both of them to come hard together.

Afterward, he dropped the buzzing wand and collapsed on top of her, drained from the experience as much as she was.

"Wow," she finally croaked.

He only grunted.

The wand continued to dance on the floor as it vibrated wildly. Sir finally lifted himself off to grab it, ripping the device from the outlet. He was covered in a sheen of sweat.

Sir slowly moved down between her legs to take a lick of her pussy, then began kissing her slick thighs. "Sweeter than I imagined. That was quite a come, babygirl."

"I almost fainted from it," she confessed.

Sir stood up sluggishly and offered her his hand. Brie took it, needing his help because she was so weak from their encounter. He led her to the couch and commanded her to spoon against him. Neither spoke for a long time, lost in the aftermath of their bliss.

Eventually, Sir nibbled her ear. "That was no vanilla fucking."

She giggled softly. "No."

"Was that what you had in mind when you chose the position?"

She turned her head toward him, a lone drop of sweat rolling down her cheek. "I hadn't thought of the wand, but yes, the sucking was definitely part of the plan."

"Well chosen," he complimented.

"The addition of the wand was genius."

He chuckled. "Having you come so hard with my cock down your throat was extremely sensual. Completely draining, but entirely worth it."

"Sooo draining, I feel like a rag doll."

He wiped the sweat from her face. "You make a delectable rag doll, babygirl."

She smiled, lifting her head to kiss him on the lips.

"My life was much duller prior to L.B.B."

"L.B.B.? I heard you mention that to Master Anderson, but I don't understand what it means."

He traced the line of her bottom lip. "Its meaning is simple. Life Before Brie."

Tears came to her eyes as she stared at Sir. There were no words for the love she felt.

Brie lay her head back down and snuggled closer, content just to be.

The Unwrapping

S ir handed Brie her journal and stated, "I would like you to write a new fantasy for me."

She grinned, knowing that such a request allowed her to share her deepest desires with him. "It would be my pleasure, Sir."

She settled herself at her desk and opened the pages with reverence. Every fantasy she'd written was dear to her and many had memories attached to them. It had been a while since she'd penned one for her Master, and she felt a thrill of excitement as she began.

Brie knew exactly what she would write about. It was directly inspired by their time on the island. She had no idea how Sir would be able to fulfill it, but it did not stop her from pouring the fantasy out on the page.

She was completely lost in the passion of the story when she felt a tap on her shoulder. "Not done yet?"

Brie shrugged, smiling up at Sir. "Now that I don't have a time limit, I can write as much as I want."

"I may have to buy you a new journal if you keep that up."

She looked up at him, feeling all tingly inside, an aftereffect of writing her fantasy down. "I'm almost done, Sir. Just a few more details to add."

"I look forward to reading it when I get back."

She put her pen down. "Back from what, Sir?"

"I just received noticed of a lucrative offer from a company in Dubai. It's too good to pass up, even though it's short notice."

"When do you leave?"

"Tomorrow evening. I need to do some heavy research and work on my presentation. It'll mean a late night tonight."

Although she hated to have him leave, she understood the importance of the trip. "I can pack for you, if you'd like. How long will you be gone?"

"That's the good news. I'll be in and out. Only staying for two days—the rest of the time will be eaten up by travel."

"I don't envy you that, Sir."

"Neither do I, but I'd rather come home than spend any more time there than necessary." He swept his hand over her shoulders as he walked past, heading toward the closet. He set out his suitcase and smiled at her. "Your help would be appreciated. Thank you."

Brie set down her journal on the desk and began picking out his favorite suits. "One belt or five?"

He chuckled. "One should do—however, lay out the other four on my nightstand. For when I get back."

"I like the way you think, Sir."

"When you're done here, come find me. I think it's time we unwrap the wedding gifts."

She giggled. "The girls were just asking about them."

"It will give you a nice distraction, writing out all those thank you notes while I'm gone."

She laughed. "Honestly, it's a lovely plan."

"Good." He nodded to her before leaving the room.

She could tell he was uneasy about leaving her so soon, but he'd always been clear that this was a part of their lives. It made no sense for her to be a big baby about it now.

While she was finishing his packing, she got a call on her cell phone. Brie was surprised to see it was Tono and answered immediately. "Hello Tono, it's so good to hear from you."

"Is everything okay, Brie?" he asked with concern in his voice.

Brie laughed. "Yes, everything is wonderful here! We made it back home just a few days ago."

"Oh…" He paused. "I am relieved to hear it. I had a dream that was disturbing. In it you were crying."

She smiled into the phone. "Well, I have been crying," she agreed but quickly added, "However, they have all been happy tears."

"I'm glad." He let out a long, drawn-out sigh. "Hearing the joy in your voice relieves me greatly."

"I can't believe you somehow sensed I was pregnant, Tono. We only found out a few days ago."

"The honeymoon was a success then."

She giggled. "Yes, and now I get to prepare for my first child. I'm feeling a bit overwhelmed. Maybe that's what you were picking up on."

He chuckled lightly. "Perhaps. Are you wishing for a

boy or a girl?"

"Honestly, I don't care as long as the baby is healthy. I want to give this little one the best future I can. I've even given up alcohol for coconut juice. Sir has as well to make it easier for me."

"Dedicated parents from the beginning. That is good to hear."

"How are you, Tono?"

She could hear the smile in his voice when he answered, "I am well, Brie."

"And Autumn?"

He chuckled again. "She is well, too."

"That's all you're going to give me?"

"We are comfortable together."

She laughed. "Well, knowing you, that speaks volumes."

"So you are good?" he reaffirmed.

"I am, Tono."

Ever thoughtful, he asked, "Should I keep the news of your pregnancy to myself?"

"No, feel free to tell Autumn. I spoke to Lea just yesterday." She giggled. "Who knows? Autumn may already know and is keeping it from you."

He laughed lightly. "It's possible."

"I'd thank you for the wedding gift, but I'm about to go open them."

"Don't let me keep you then."

She pressed the phone hard against her cheek. "Thank you for checking up on me. I appreciate that you cared enough to call."

"That connection will remain, even as our lives

change with the current."

"It is a comfort to me, Tono."

"To me as well, Brie."

She ended the call, feeling a sense of harmony with him, with Sir, with the baby—and the whole wide world. "I think I am going to love being a mom."

Brie left the bedroom and found Sir at his desk. He was reading a business letter, but as soon as he saw her, Sir folded it up and proceeded to slowly rip the letter into tiny pieces, throwing it in the trash when he was done.

"Is everything all right?"

"Unfortunately, there's a legal matter I must address. Nothing that concerns you, however."

"Are you having issues with one of your clients?"

Sir stood up, taking a deep breath and forcing a smile. "As I said, it doesn't concern you. Don't give it a second thought."

Brie stared at the trash can, wondering why he'd been so thorough in tearing it up.

"Confidentiality is of upmost importance in this matter," he explained as if reading her mind. Sir held up the silk pouch Brie had worn during the dance on her wedding day. "Are you ready to begin the festivities, babygirl?"

She grinned. "Now this is the kind of assignment I love."

"I was surprised you didn't insist on doing it first thing once we returned home—knowing how you are about presents."

Brie stood on her tiptoes to kiss him. "Actually, dear

husband, I've been too distracted by you to care."

They settled onto the couch and Brie reached to pull out the first envelope. "It's from your cousin Benito." She broke open the seal and was shocked to find three hundred dollars inside. "So much?"

"Think of it as being similar to the Japanese *koden*. Italians are generous at weddings, and he is good family."

Brie wrote down the amount on the envelope and put it aside for thank you notes later.

She pulled out Master Anderson's thick envelope next. "What in the heck could this be?"

"I have no idea."

Brie forced the folded paper out and opened it up. She instantly began laughing as she handed it over to Sir. It was a picture of a bare-chested Master Anderson holding Cayenne with the words *What do you give the couple who has everything? A date to weed with us in the buff!* written across it.

Sir shook his head and laughed.

Brie giggled, "He must want to initiate his new neighbors in grand style."

"I'll remember this when he marries."

"Do you think he ever will?"

"Brad's a cowboy at heart. He's always wanted what his parents have—but not in Greeley. Have you ever met his parents?"

"No, I've never had the pleasure."

"They're good country folk. Friendly, welcoming, would give you the shirts off their backs…"

"So that's where he gets that from."

"Funny," Sir chuckled. "I do believe his fascination

with plants comes from his childhood in the country."

"Interesting."

"His parents took me in as an honorary member of his family when I was in college. I spent several weekends on their ranch. Although Brad's distanced himself from his humble beginnings, I see the best part of them in him."

Brie looked back down at the picture. "That's beautiful, Sir."

"We all have histories that shape our lives, but most are unaware of it."

Brie pulled out Tono's envelope next. She kissed the painted flower before opening it. Inside was five hundred dollars and a note.

A solemn vow of support

Given to my chosen family

Tear welled up in her eyes.

"Nosaka is one of the few men I admire. He exudes a gentle countenance, but in truth he has the fortitude of a thousand men."

"I'm truly touched," she said, holding back the tears as she placed the card back inside the envelope, silently vowing to find a special place for it later.

Brie pulled many more small envelopes from Sir's side of the family, each containing from one hundred to four hundred dollars. She shook her head looking at the pile of loot they'd amassed.

"What are we going to do with all this money?"

"I suggest we clear out the guest room and start a

nursery."

She looked down at the cash with a grateful heart. His family's generosity would become a part of their child's future. How beautiful was that?

"You're not finished," he reminded her.

She laughed at herself getting all sentimental when there were still gifts to open. Brie pulled out Master Coen's envelope next. She opened it to find two plane tickets to Australia with open dates, as well as a short note.

Come Down Under ASAP

"I guess we have no excuse not to visit," she told Sir with a grin.

Sir's eyes twinkled. "I've always want to travel there. Serious trouble to explore…"

She placed the tickets on the coffee table and scribbled down tickets on the envelope, placing it with the rest. Next Brie pulled out the silver envelope Marquis Gray had given her.

Instead of money, he had written something on the little card.

The Gift of a Traditional Thai Cooking Class for Two
(Tomato and egg dishes are lacking)

"How thoughtful," Brie said, handing it to Sir with a grin.

"That actually is a good idea." He put his arm around her. "Should be fun sharing a new cuisine with you."

Brie didn't want to tell him how patient Boa had been with her. Cooking did not come naturally to Brie, even though she had succeeded in nailing down several of Sir's favorite dishes with Boa's help. "It should be…an interesting experience."

She pulled out Baron's envelope next. It was vivid red, and she'd remembered his devilish smile when he'd handed it to her. She held it up, remarking, "I'm really curious about this one, but I think you should open it."

He took it from her, breaking the seal and sliding out the card. Sir tilted his head after reading it. Without saying a word, he handed to it her.

An invitation to teach

"Well, that's a mystery…" Brie mused. "I do remember he mentioned that he wanted us to come visit his new home when we got back."

Sir stroked his chin as he considered its meaning. "I wonder what Baron is up to."

"I'm not sure but, based on the conversation I had at breakfast, Captain is somehow involved."

"Hmm…the plot thickens."

As if by fate, she picked Captain's card next. "Do you think we'll get another clue?"

"Open it," Sir ordered, obviously curious.

She slipped out the card and was surprised to find two gift certificates for a hot air balloon ride. She grabbed onto Sir's arm. "That sounds fun!"

"Entertaining yes, but no additional clue to Baron's gift."

"Unless, of course, they plant to start a new kink. BDSM Ballooning—take your kink to a higher level," Brie said, laughing. She reached back in to fish out one of the few remaining envelopes and pulled out Mr. Gallant's.

Cash is customary but too impersonal for a couple
we both esteem
Our gift to the newlyweds
A jump off the Bridge to Nowhere
Enjoy

A gift card was included, reserving a bungee jump for two.

"That's an experience," Sir replied.

"You've been?"

"With Rytsar."

"I can just imagine the two of you egging each other on." When Brie thought about it, however, her heart started racing. Actually jumping from a bridge…

Although she had been willing to take an emotional leap for love, this took a totally different kind of courage. "What's it like, Sir?"

He took the gift card from her and tucked it in his wallet. "I don't want to spoil it for you. Although I do look forward to seeing the look on your face just before you jump and the one after they pull you back up."

Brie shivered. "What if the bungee breaks?"

"They've never had an injury in all the years they've been open, so you can let go of that fear."

"That's definitely a relief," she sighed. But another

cold shiver ran down her spine at the thought of falling into the darkness.

She pulled out an envelope that only read "Brianna and Thane". Curious, she opened it up and felt her heart melt when she saw it was from her parents. It touched her deeply that it was written in her father's illegible handwriting. Being his child, however, it was readable to her.

Brianna and Thane,

We have gifted you the anniversary clock my parents gave us on our wedding day. As you might remember, little girl, it has a special place in my heart. I kept the ridiculously large thing with me when we were separated to remind me that every minute I was away from my family was one minute closer to my return. It saw me through some difficult days. We hope it provides you with comfort in the years to come.

There is hope in every minute.

* Marquis Gray has graciously agreed to hold the gift until your return.

Brie was overwhelmed by the gift and explained to Thane, "I told you once that my dad had trouble finding a job after the Darius incident. He was forced to leave us behind to seek employment in another state. Mom and I had to live in a homeless shelter while he traveled from state to state searching for work that could support our family."

Brie sighed, those difficult memories still vivid in her mind. "I remember the look on my dad's face the day he left us behind. He was the strength in our family, but that day he looked like a defeated man. It scared me. Before he drove off, he held up the anniversary clock to show my mother and promised us both he would be back as soon as he had a job."

The pain of that season in her life washed over Brie like a tidal wave and she choked out, "I can't believe they gave this to us. It means so much to them."

Sir held her close. "As a parent it's natural to pass on what is most valuable to you."

Brie nodded her head.

"We will get your family clock from Marquis Gray as soon as I return from Dubai."

"I would love that, Sir."

Sir retrieved the next envelope. "This appears to be from Samantha."

"Oh, I remember Lea slipped that in before Rytsar whisked me off."

He opened it and a thousand-dollar bill fell out. Brie picked it up and stared at it in disbelief. "I didn't know they made such a thing."

"They don't anymore," Sir told her, fascinated by the unusual bill. "If I recall right, they stopped making them in the 1940s." Sir held the card for both of them to read.

> *Sir Davis, my friend and mentor, I owe you a thousand times over.*
>
> *Sending my love and good-tidings to you both*

on this auspicious day.
I hope to celebrate with you personally
someday soon.
~Samantha

Brie could hear the sadness behind the words in her note. She felt certain Ms. Clark had wanted to be a part of their big day, but had chosen to stay behind so Rytsar could stand as best man without fear of seeing her.

"We should visit Denver soon," Brie stated.

"It would be a good weekend trip," Sir agreed, staring at the bill. "A gift like that deserves a personal thank you."

"I believe there is one more left in here," Brie said, shaking the silk bag. She couldn't help smiling because she knew it had to be Rytsar's. "Last time he gave me a cabin. What do you think he did this time?"

Sir said nothing.

"You already know, don't you?" Brie accused, bumping against him.

"It required my input. So yes, dear wife, I already know what it is."

"And you kept it from me all this time?"

"Rytsar insisted."

"Ah, then I can't fault you. I'm sorry, Sir."

"Apology accepted," he acquiesced but pinched her on the ass as penance, making her giggle. "Now go ahead and open it."

Brie noticed that his smirk grew into a boyish smile as he stared at the sealed envelope, waiting for her to comply.

Her curiosity further heightened, Brie tore open the envelope and read the card with just two words on it.

The Isle

"Sir?"

"It was a mutual investment between he and I. He started construction plans the day after I proposed to you."

"It's ours?"

"Yes, all three of us own that island."

She stared at the card, completely stunned.

"As I'm sure you already suspect, he plans to join us the next time we visit."

She felt the butterflies start. Sir *and* Rytsar alone with her on a deserted island? *OMG!*

"I can tell by the expression on your face that you are pleased."

She leaned against him. "And a little frightened, to be honest."

"As you should be. He and I have been talking."

She looked up at him, smiling nervously. "Will it hurt?"

"Most definitely."

Brie squeaked but she felt a thrill of excitement. To be tested by these two Doms was an honor and challenge, but the sex...oh, the sex! She burned with desire thinking back on their times together.

"Naturally, that won't be for a while now that you're pregnant."

Brie slumped on the couch. "Dang!"

Sir laughed. "It gives you an opportunity to practice patience."

She frowned. "It's not my strong suit."

"Which is why it must be tested time and time again."

She fanned herself with the card. "I guess I'll be fantasizing about that island for a long time."

"Join the club, babygirl. Rytsar and I have been fantasizing alone long enough."

Cold Reality

S ir had his suitcase set beside the door. Brie helped him with his jacket in preparation of his departure, disappointed that she was not allowed to go to the airport. He had insisted she stay home rather than seeing him off there as she normally did.

"I'd rather have you safe at home than fighting LA traffic."

"I understand," she'd agreed, although she felt he was being *way* overprotective. However…it was sweet. Knowing he cared so much about her and the baby was endearing, so Brie decided for the time being to honor his need to protect her so fiercely.

He picked up the suitcase and was about to open the door when he suddenly stopped. Sir turned to Brie, slowly setting the suitcase back down. "Before I leave, there are two things I must do."

He returned to her. "It's only right I give you a proper goodbye, Mrs. Davis." Sir fisted her hair, pulling her head back to plant an impassioned kiss on her lips.

She moaned softly in pleasure. "Thank you, Mr. Davis. I like proper goodbyes."

Sir then got down on his knees and held her waist with both hands as he pressed his lips against her stomach. "Goodbye, little one."

Brie's heart melted into a puddle.

Sir stood up and looked at her tenderly. "I'll be back soon."

"Knowing you're coming back in four days makes this parting so much easier."

"I agree." He picked up his suitcase again and opened the door, glancing back once as he waited for the elevator. Brie blew him a kiss, totally and utterly in love with the man.

When the elevator closed, she shut the door, sighing in contentment still feeling the lingering ghost of his kiss on her tummy.

"I love you, Thane," she said out loud, smiling to herself as she went to her desk to begin the task of writing the stack of thank-you notes that were needed. She actually enjoyed the project because it allowed her to reflect on that beautiful day and each person who'd joined them to celebrate.

After several hours at it, her eyes became blurry. Deciding a break was in order, Brie headed to the bedroom to slip into her favorite PJs. Then she made her way to the kitchen to microwave a fresh bowl of popcorn.

Brie snuggled up on the couch, placing the bowl between her crossed legs. She suspected it wouldn't be long before crossing her legs was a thing of the past and that made her smile.

Grabbing the remote, she turned on the TV wanting

to indulge in an old black-and-white movie. To her delight, the cable station had just started playing *Gone with the Wind*. She rubbed her belly and cooed to her unborn child. "Someday you will understand the dynamic between Rhett Butler and Scarlett. He not only loves her deeply, but he knows how to love her *well*. I must confess I think that's one reason I love this movie so much. Scarlett may be a strong woman, but Rhett is an equally formidable man and together they make fireworks." Brie bent down closer to her stomach and added in a whisper, "Just like your daddy and me."

Brie took delight in watching Scarlett's many suitors try to win her over at the picnic. It gave her an idea, so she paused the movie and grabbed her cell phone. She called Sir, smiling when it transferred her directly to voicemail and she heard his authoritative voice asking the caller to leave a message. Since she knew he'd be flying for an extended amount of time, she thought she'd leave Sir a fun little message to greet him when he arrived at his destination.

In a playful tone she began, "So, Sir, have you ever considered roleplaying Rhett Butler? I'm watching *Gone with the Wind* right now and thought how fun it would be to get all dressed up in a poofy dress and let you hike my skirt up and spank my frilly ass." She giggled as she hung up, secretly hoping he'd take her up on the suggestion.

Sir as Rhett Butler—that was all kinds of yummy.

She resumed the movie, eating up every moment, totally savoring the part where Rhett bids for Scarlett at the charity dance.

"Oh Rhett…"

She was startled when there was a knock at the door.

Brie put the movie on pause. Since she wasn't expecting anyone, she quietly crept up to the door and looked through the peephole. To her relief she saw it was Captain and Candy. She figured Mary must have grown some balls and given Captain a call, so she unlocked the door and swung it open. "Hey, you guys! What an unexpected surprise."

Captain's look was grave and Candy seemed pensive as they entered.

"Don't worry, Mary already told me what going on with her. Both Lea and I suggested she call you."

"This isn't about Mary," Captain stated.

Brie grimaced, realizing she'd just put her foot in her mouth. Mary was so going to kill her. "Umm…forget I said anything."

"Brie, I think you should sit down," Candy suggested, leading her toward the couch.

"What's this about? You guys are starting to scare me."

Captain stood before her, a look of compassion on his war-scarred face. "We have some disturbing news, but I need you to focus on what I am about to say."

Brie stopped breathing when Candy grabbed her hand, knowing it was bad.

"There has been a plane crash at LAX. Sir Davis mentioned to me that he was taking a flight to Dubai. I've been able to confirm he *was* on the flight that went down."

Brie's whole body began to tremble uncontrollably.

"Brianna," he stated firmly. "There are survivors.

Although I can't confirm if he is one of them, *that* is what you must focus on right now."

"What happened?" she whispered.

"Since the plane was a non-stop flight, it had a full tank of fuel, which is why it burst into flames upon impact. From what they've pieced together at this point, the pilot radioed that they were experiencing a malfunction just after takeoff. They turned around attempting to land but were unsuccessful."

Brie was tormented by the fact she hadn't felt anything when his plane went down. Had he been calling out to her just before impact? She closed her eyes, forcing herself to focus—not allowing her mind to take her there.

"First, we need you to get dressed. Then I'll drive you to the hospital that's receiving survivors."

Candy guided Brie down the hallway to help her change while Captain started making phone calls.

"He's alive, Brie. I'm sure of it…" Candy said encouragingly.

Brie nodded, in too much shock to speak.

Candy was gentle but efficient getting Brie redressed, tossing her pajamas on the bed as she marched Brie out of the room. "We're ready, Captain."

He looked at Brie somberly. "I know this is hard—the not knowing—but you must be strong. There is no point entertaining what-if's until you know the truth of the situation. Even then, no matter what the news, Sir Davis would expect you to be courageous for the health of the baby."

Brie only nodded, glancing briefly down at her small

belly. The thought of the baby losing his father was too overwhelming, and the tears began to fall.

"Don't, Mrs. Davis. We know nothing right now. It serves no purpose to weep about the unknown."

She wiped away her tears and closed her eyes until she had control over her emotions again. She understood the reality of what she must do, even though every cell in her body wanted to run away.

Opening her eyes again, Brie stated simply, "Sir needs me."

"Yes, he does, Mrs. Davis," Captain agreed.

Brie straightened her stance, pushing back her shoulders as she waited for the elevator. Captain was right; it was foolish to worry about what might be when Sir was lying in the hospital, needing her by his side.

She was eternally grateful for Captain once they made it to their destination. The lobby of the hospital was pure mayhem, with first-responders, concerned family members and the press milling about. It took his dogged determination and forthright spirit to get the answers they needed to begin the search to see if Sir was among the living.

"It appears that there are two men brought in who match Sir Davis' approximate age," Captain explained.

Brie held her breath as she was escorted to the first room. The chaos of the hospital only added to her building anxiety. The attendant told her as they walked down the hallway, "We have two types of patients from this crash—burn victims and blunt trauma victims due to the back end separating from the plane upon contact."

Brie was the only allowed into the first hospital room

after scrubbing down and donning protective clothing. She walked in to find a man covered in a plastic tent to protect him from infection due to his extensive burns. Brie approached cautiously, quelling the need to cry out when she saw just how extensive the burns really were. The man's face was blackened and unrecognizable, no hair left after contacting the intense heat of the jet fuel.

"Look at other parts of his body. See if there are any distinguishing marks you recognize," the attendant advised her.

Tears ran down Brie's face as she looked the poor man over. His hands had been burned as well. Only his chest seemed free from the effects of the fire. Brie drew closer, praying she would not find what she was looking for…

She sucked in her breath when she noted his chest was free of the brand. *Thank God…* Brie felt almost guilty for feeling relieved it was not Sir, knowing that some other family would have to bear the pain of this tragedy.

In a bare whisper she informed the attendant that it was not her husband, but she put her gloved hand on the plastic and said a single prayer. "Mercy…"

Brie was taken out of the room, where she removed her gloves, booties and gown. A nurse took them from her, a look of empathy in her green eyes.

Brie was escorted to a different floor, down a long corridor. "Just as before, you will need to look for distinguishing marks. This patient is suffering from major brain trauma."

She walked into the room with extreme trepidation.

Either this patient was Sir or her husband was among the dead. She walked up to the bed hesitantly, hoping with everything in her that she would find it was Sir, despite the man's serious condition. His body was covered in tubes and bandages, making it impossible to see his face or chest. It left her little to go by, but she studied his left hand. Not only did it lack her ring, it was small and thin—not the hand of her Master.

Brie could not hold back the sob that escaped her lips. "It's not him."

"I'm so sorry, Mrs. Davis."

Brie only shook her head as she left the room, all hope lost.

Captain took her into his stiff but protective embrace. "Our job is not done until we find him, Mrs. Davis."

She nodded, even though the thought of going to the morgue terrified her.

Captain guided Brie into Candy's arms, stating, "Let me talk to the staff before we leave."

Candy squeezed Brie tightly, saying nothing.

It was a relief to her, because there was nothing to be said—her world had imploded in the blink of an eye.

Captain came back shortly, taking Brie by the arm and leading her out of the chaos and pain of the hospital. But Brie understood he was taking her from a place of life and hope to a place of death.

"I can't..." Brie whimpered.

"You will," Captain insisted. "He deserves no less."

Brie slumped in the seat, numb to the core of her being as he drove them ever closer to the death of her soul. She pressed her head against the window, wishing she could disappear.

Captain's phone rang but his words were muffled and far away as she retreated further into herself.

"Mrs. Davis...Mrs. Davis!" he repeated more loudly, shaking her to get her attention.

Brie turned her head to him listlessly, resentful he was forcing her back into reality.

"There were a handful of survivors that were transported to a different hospital. We are heading there now."

Brie's lip trembled, not trusting she'd heard him correctly. "More survivors?"

"Yes," Candy answered excitedly. "Captain says there was a second group of survivors found farther from the crash site. They were ejected when the back of the plane split in two."

Hope.

Even though it invited more pain, Brie held on to the belief Sir was there. She sat up, wiping her face clean of tears. She didn't want him to know she'd given up on him being alive.

There was much less activity as they made their way through the lobby of the new hospital. Only a handful of survivors had been sent there and the press had yet to descend on the place.

Brie was told there was only one man fitting Sir's description from the crash. The man was in critical but stable condition. Brie walked toward the room, knowing her fate lay on the other side of the door—either blessed relief or complete desolation.

The nurse opened it for her, guiding Brie inside but staying in the doorway as Brie approached the bed.

The first thing Brie noticed was the dark hair jutting out from the white bandages covering his forehead. The sheer abundance of bandages and wires, as well as the breathing tube keeping him alive were frightening, but when her gaze fell onto his hand and she saw the dark band on his finger she broke out in hysterical laughter. "You're alive!"

Brie began kissing Sir on every exposed piece of flesh, the ache of hope bursting through her darkness.

The nurse came over to stop her frenzied kisses. "Mrs. Davis, are you positive this is Thane Davis?"

"Yes!" She moved closer, looking at Sir's serene expression covered in tubes and wires and suddenly felt a cold chill.

He looked exactly like his mother. Had the wretch come back from the dead to exact her unwarranted vengeance on her son?

Brie shook off the feeling of déjà vu, determined that his fate would not be the same.

"I will get the doctor so she can fill you in on his current condition," the nurse stated.

Brie threw her arms around her and cried tearfully, "Thank you."

The woman smiled when Brie let go. "I'm grateful you have been reunited with your husband, Mrs. Davis."

"I lost hope after visiting the other hospital. I was heading to the morgue when we got the call to come here."

The nurse only nodded, keeping her emotions in

check. Brie understood that the staff would be facing the devastation of many families who would not be so lucky. "Can my friends come in?"

"I'm sorry, only close family are allowed in Intensive Care."

It forced Brie to leave Sir's side so she could inform her friends about the wondrous news. She took his limp hand in hers and kissed it tenderly. "I'll be right back, Sir."

She found Captain and Candy in the waiting room and quietly shared the happy news, acutely aware that other families were there hoping to find their loved ones but would not be as fortunate.

"How is he, Brie?" Candy asked.

"He's in critical condition, but *alive*. The doctor is coming to speak with me so I have to hurry back."

"But he is stable," Captain stated, wanting to confirm.

She looked at him gratefully. "Yes, Captain. I want to thank you for bringing me here…" Her voice failed her for a moment. She swallowed down the lump in her throat. "Thank you for giving me my world back."

In a spontaneous gesture of joy, she kissed his scarred cheek. It was unorthodox and against his protocol, but she could not stop herself.

He cleared his throat. "As I said before, Mrs. Davis, it is never wise to concern ourselves with what-ifs. I'm relieved Sir Davis survived, but now you must concentrate on his recovery."

"Yes…" she smiled, nodding happily as tears of relief rolled down her cheeks.

He looked down at her stomach for emphasis, "Your child needs his father to be well."

Brie caressed her tummy lovingly. "Yes."

"Brie, is there anyone you want me to call while you talk to the doctor?" Candy offered.

Brie handed Candy her phone. "Please call my parents, and the Reynolds. That's all for now—until I learn more. But if either Lea or Mary call, you have my permission to answer and tell them what's happened."

She was almost out the door when she suddenly remembered Tono. She felt a prickling down her spine when she recalled their last conversation. Had he foreseen this?

"If Tono Nosaka calls, please let him know Sir is alive and I am fine."

Brie didn't want to contemplate how Tono could have known, because it would lead her into questions of whether or not she could have done something to prevent what happened. The what-ifs would have to wait. Right now, she needed to concentrate solely on Sir's health and recovery.

When Brie returned she found the nurse still waiting with him. "The doctor was just here, but said she would return."

Brie wrung her hands anxiously. "I'm sorry I missed her. I needed to let my family know he's alive."

The nurse put her hand on Brie's arm. "Dr. Hessen understands. When dealing with the wounded, she believes it is her duty to care not only for her patient, but the loved ones as well."

Brie felt the tears threaten again and took a deep

breath. She moved back to Sir's side. Nothing had changed. His heartbeat was unusually slow but steady, the look on his face calm and unconcerned even though his body was a mass of bandages, tubes, wires and a large cast on his leg.

Dr. Hessen returned a few minutes later. The woman looked to be of Indian descent. She wore a kind but tense smile on her lips when she addressed Brie. "It is good to meet you, Mrs. Davis. We were hoping his family would come soon."

"How is he?"

The doctor pushed her glasses up on the bridge of her nose. "The news is grave, but he is stable at the moment. Mr. Davis has severe head trauma, several broken ribs, and a shattered femur. The ribs and the leg will heal with time, but the head injury is concerning."

"What's being done for him?"

"We are closely monitoring Mr. Davis. It's important we relieve any bleeding or swelling of the brain. The injury to his skull is our number one concern right now."

"What can I do?" Brie pleaded, needing a task to focus on.

Dr. Hessen smiled. "Keep talking to him, Mrs. Davis, and if you are so inclined, ask friends and family members to pray. At this moment, we must rely on time and the human body's power to heal."

Brie frowned, looking back at Sir. "I wonder what happened. How did he survive when others did not?"

Dr. Hessen nodded toward the door. "Nurse Abby, could you take Mrs. Davis to the children's wing?"

The nurse smiled. "Of course."

Brie looked at the doctor questioningly.

"I believe there's something you should see," Dr. Hessen told her.

Abby led Brie to another wing of the hospital where the walls were painted with bright colored animals.

Pointing through the small window of a hospital door, the nurse shared, "That little girl was found with your husband's arms wrapped around her. At first it was assumed they were related. From what I was told, he saved her life. I don't know the details, but the first-responders might."

Brie stood silently looking through the window. The little girl lying in the bed was probably no older than six. A woman, most likely the mother, was hovering over her constantly wiping away her tears as she smiled down at the child.

Brie understood the woman's relief at being given a second chance with her daughter. It gave Brie comfort and a sense of pride to know that Sir had protected this child as the last possible act of his life.

"Thank you, Abby."

"Dr. Hessen felt it was important that you know."

Abby guided Brie back to Sir's room. Brie entered alone and approached him slowly, overwhelmed with visions of both Tono's father and Sir's own mother as they lay dying in hospital beds.

That would not be Sir's fate!

She leaned over and lightly laid her ear on his chest to listen to his heart beat. It was the only thing she could hold on to—that steady, unending heartbeat of the man she loved with every ounce of her being.

Brie took his hand and held it tightly. When standing became too much, she pulled over a chair and sat down, grasping his hand again. The beeping of the heart monitor her only communication with Sir.

Eventually Abby came in and informed her, "Your friends are asking for you."

Brie glanced at the clock, realizing just how many hours had passed. "They're still here?" Brie looked back at Sir and shook her head. "Please tell them they can go home now. I'll be fine."

Abby chuckled. "The older gentleman warned me you would say that. He told me to insist you come out to meet with them."

Brie normally was not one to disobey a respected Dom, but she refused again. "Please tell them Sir is stable and I need to remain by his side."

Abby replied almost apologetically, "He told me to bring up the baby if you refused."

Brie sighed, but conceded that Captain had won the battle of wills. She kissed Sir's hand. "Captain is being stubborn, but I won't be long."

Brie followed the nurse out and met Captain and Candy just outside the doors of the ICU.

Candy instantly gave Brie a hug. Brie welcomed the energy Candy passed on through that simple connection.

"Have you had anything to drink since coming here, Mrs. Davis?" Captain asked.

She shook her head. "No, but that's not what's important right now."

"Staying hydrated *is* important, especially when you're with child," he corrected.

Brie felt her ire rise.

Captain read it on her face and advised her, "While stubbornness can be a noble characteristic, Mrs. Davis, it isn't when it affects your health or the health of the child you carry."

Brie found it ironic that he was calling *her* stubborn. "There's no need to worry about me. Sir is the only one we should be focusing on. You said that yourself."

Candy replied kindly, "We both agree that caring for him is important, Brie, but Captain's right that you need to take care of yourself." She took Brie's hand. "So we're going to get you something to eat and drink."

"I'm not thirsty or hungry," Brie insisted.

Captain asked with a knowing look, "What did you eat for dinner?"

Brie sighed, knowing her answer would displease him. "Popcorn."

"Don't forget that baby needs you even more than Sir Davis does," he insisted with a hint of compassion in his voice.

Brie wanted to disagree, but the concerned look in his eyes kept her silent. She looked back at the doors of the ICU as she was led away.

I'm coming right back, Sir, she silently promised.

Captain was not satisfied with what the hospital cafeteria had to offer and took them to an offsite café. He wouldn't even let Brie order, getting her a large salad with plenty of chicken, a glass of milk, and an additional glass of water.

She looked at the large salad bowl and laughed. "There is no way I can eat all this."

"You're not leaving until it is all gone, Mrs. Davis," Captain stated firmly.

Brie sighed, feeling like a child. She hated every minute she was away from Sir, but knew Captain would not relent, so she started scarfing it down. The more she consumed, however, the more she realized how much she'd needed to eat. By the time she was done, she looked at Captain feeling foolish.

"Thank you, Captain. I…" She patted her belly. "*We* needed that."

"Of course you did. It's important that you remember that in the weeks ah—."

"No," Brie interrupted. "Sir will wake up any minute, I'm sure of it. Several times I swore he was about to open his eyes." She couldn't help smiling when she told them, "That's why I can't stay here long, I need to get back. I *have* to be the first person he sees when he wakes up."

Captain put his hand on hers. "I understand, Mrs. Davis, but you cannot forsake your health in your desire to be there for your Master."

Brie smiled as she stood up and promised solemnly, "I will make a sincere effort, Captain." She gave Candy a quick hug. "Please go home and get rest yourselves." She added before racing out the door, "Thank you both. I'll be calling you soon with good news."

"God willing," Captain answered.

Brie felt energized when she headed back into the hospital, certain Sir would awaken upon her return.

She quickly realized nothing had changed when she entered his room. It was silent except for the contestant beeping of the heart monitor. However, she didn't let it discourage her. Brie stood next to the bed, taking his hand again. "I'm back, Sir, just like I promised." She glanced at the heart monitor hoping to see a change, some indication that he'd heard her—that he knew she was there.

It remained steady and unchanging.

"That's okay," she assured him, grabbing the chair to sit closer. "You just need a little more time to heal."

The Reynolds came to the room not long after.

"How's he doing, Brie?" Mr. Reynolds asked, his voice heavy with concern. He walked up to stand beside her next to the bed.

"He's suffered a bad head injury and is in a coma. As you can see, he has broken bones too. They have him on a breathing tube, but will take that out when he wakes up."

"When do they think that will be, dear?" Judy asked.

"The doctor can't say."

Mr. Reynolds wrapped his arm around Brie. "He's a fighter."

She nodded. "I know he is."

"Is there anything we can do for you?" Judy asked, moving to the other side of Brie to add her hug and support.

"No, not really. We just have to wait and pray."

"Have you called Master Anderson?" Mr. Reynolds asked. "I'm certain the Training Center staff would want to know what's happened."

"I haven't called anyone. Candy took care of contacting you and my parents."

"Then let me help you with that," Judy offered. "Who would you like me to call?"

Brie handed her the phone. "Just our closest friends."

When Judy looked unsure, Mr. Reynolds told his wife, "I can help with that."

"Thank you both," Brie murmured, looking down at Sir. "I really don't have the heart to talk to anyone right now."

Mr. Reynolds squeezed her tighter. "Quite understandable. You need to concentrate on Thane, and we'll take care of the rest."

She turned and buried her head on his shoulder. "I almost lost him…"

Mr. Reynolds held her even tighter. "Thane's a fighter, Brie. He'll survive this."

Brie looked back at Sir again. "He hasn't moved this entire time. No change, nothing."

Mr. Reynolds turned to face her. "I remember when Thane was a boy. We were all together at the lake one summer, Judy, myself, Ruth, Alonzo, and Thane. Being an adventurous boy of ten, he decided to jump in the water—Thane has always had an affinity for water. Anyway, he somehow got trapped by old baling wire that had been discarded years ago.

"God only knows how long he was down there before Alonzo noticed he hadn't come up for air. He dived in, and I followed. It took both of us to untangle Thane, but by the time we got him to the surface he'd stopped breathing."

Mr. Reynolds took a ragged breath. "I will never forget the fear when I realized Thane was gone. Luckily, Judy knew CPR. She kept pumping his chest and didn't stop until he coughed up water."

Brie just shook her head, having never heard the story.

"Thane talked to me about it after," Mr. Reynolds continued. "Told me when he'd gotten tangled up in the wire he'd started to panic, but the more he struggled the more ensnared he became. Thane said there came a point when he knew he could take a deep breath and die peacefully or keep fighting to live. He chose to keep fighting, and that's when he felt our hands on him."

Mr. Reynolds snorted, shaking his head as he smiled to himself. "The very next day, I found him back in the water. That boy doesn't shy away from a fight." He squeezed Brie hard. "Thane won't give up now. He has too much to live for."

One of the men who had been the first to respond to the crash site requested to speak with Brie. She reluctantly left Sir's side, wanting to thank the person who'd helped save his life.

The tall man with a decidedly Grecian look held out his hand to her. "It is an honor to meet the wife of the hero."

"The honor is mine. How can I ever repay you for saving my husband's life?"

"I did nothing more than to keep him still until the

ambulance arrived." Tears came to his dark eyes when he explained, "When I saw his white shirt out in the field, I realized we'd found another one. I had no idea at the time…"

"What?" she asked breathlessly, desperate to know what the man had seen.

"I thought he was alone. It wasn't until I tried to get his vitals that I realized there was a little girl underneath him, clutched protectively in his arms."

Brie's bottom lip trembled as he continued.

"I naturally assumed he was the girl's father, but after speaking to the child's family it was clear that that was not the case."

Brie smiled sadly, looking down at her stomach. "He will be a father—soon."

His eyes widened in understanding. "Oh, I see." He looked at her with compassion. "The family of the little girl is overflowing with gratitude and wanted me to ask if they could speak to you privately."

"Me? But why?"

"Lucinda, the little girl he saved, is well enough that she'll be leaving the hospital tomorrow. It's a true miracle. They had hoped to thank Mr. Davis personally, but under the circumstances they would like to speak to you before they go."

Brie looked back in the direction of Sir's room, moved by his bravery. It was in honor of him that she agreed to leave his side to follow the man back to Lucinda's hospital room.

The young girl was smiling when Brie entered, but as soon as she saw a stranger, the girl instantly became shy and looked away. Brie understood and took the focus off Lucinda by addressing the woman she had observed the previous day.

"Hello, I'm Brie Davis, Thane's wife."

The woman held out her hand to Brie, clasping it tightly. "Hello, Brie. I'm Dorothy Jefferys. These are my parents and of course this is my daughter, Lucinda."

Brie nodded at the older couple and smiled at the shy girl.

"I can't begin to tell you how grateful we are to your husband. Not only did he protect my baby when the plane went down, but she told me that he helped calm her even before they took off."

"Did he?" Brie asked, touched by her words.

"Yes. Lucinda was alone on the flight headed to visit her father in Sharjah. I was sick with worry knowing my child was flying overseas by herself, but it couldn't be helped. And then…when I heard…" Mrs. Jefferys glanced at her daughter briefly, fighting back the tears.

Lucinda looked up at her mother with concern.

Clearing her throat, Dorothy finished with a simple, "Naturally, I was distraught."

Brie nodded, remembering her own terror the moment she realized Sir had been involved in the plane crash. "I hear you're doing okay," Brie said in a cheery voice, smiling at Lucinda.

The girl held up her arm, which was covered in a neon pink cast. "It's pink."

Her mother added, "The doctors are amazed she walked away with only a broken arm and a few scrapes." Dorothy became emotional when she explained, "We owe it all to your husband."

"The nice man helped me!" Lucinda piped up. "I was scared, but he told me I was brave and would be okay."

"The paramedics informed us your husband covered Lucinda with his body when the plane went down. Miraculously, Lucinda doesn't remember anything after the initial takeoff."

Brie closed her eyes, nodding to acknowledge what Dorothy had shared, but trying her best to keep the tears at bay for the girl's sake. Once she had her emotions in check, she looked at Lucinda again and smiled.

It was a blessing the girl couldn't remember the horrors of the crash. Brie wondered if Sir would be equally as lucky when he awakened. How must he have felt knowing he was going to die—never to see Brie again or hold their unborn child?

Sir had faced death by helping another. It spoke volumes about the man.

"I wish there was more I could give you than a simple thank you," Dorothy replied.

"A thank you is all my husband would have accepted," Brie assured her.

"I made him this!" Lucinda announced, waving a picture of two stick figures. One tiny one with yellow curls and one big one with a straight line of brown on top of its head. She'd drawn a rainbow above them.

"Would you like me to give it to him?" Brie asked.

Lucinda hugged the picture to herself. "No."

Brie chuckled at her frankness. "I bet you want to give it to him yourself, don't you?"

The girl nodded her head vigorously.

"When he wakes up you can give him your pretty picture. I know it will make him very happy."

The little girl gave her a self-satisfied grin.

"Is there anything we can do, Mrs. Davis? Anything at all?" Dorothy asked.

Brie thought for a moment. "Prayers for my husband would be appreciated. The doctor said prayers and time is what he needs right now."

"I will let my church know to add him to the prayer list."

"Thank you."

"Is there anything we can do for you?" the grandfather asked.

Brie shook her head. "No, I have everything I need. My husband survived."

Dorothy nodded in understanding. "We're the lucky ones."

"Yes, "Brie agreed sadly. "Not everyone was so fortunate."

"Mommy, why is the lady sad?"

Brie answered for Dorothy. "I'm just sad because my husband doesn't get to leave the hospital tomorrow like you, and he doesn't have a pink cast."

Lucinda stared joyfully at her cast. "Really pink."

"The pinkiest," Brie agreed with a smile.

Brie left the little family with a lighter heart. It made it much easier when she returned to Sir's room and was hit by how still he was. Focusing on the present, she spent time sharing with him about Lucinda and her family. She also spoke about his bravery and sacrifice. "I'm so proud, Sir. Even in the darkest moment, you showed the world who you really are."

She stood up and looked down at him. Leaning in to kiss his cheek, she whispered, "Come back to me."

Condors

In the days that followed, Brie saw absolutely no change in Sir's condition. Dr. Hessen assured her that was a good sign. "His body is healing. Every day he doesn't suffer from a setback is a step forward."

Brie took the opportunity, with permission from the doctor, to fill Sir's room with sound. She brought Alonzo's music and played it, hoping his father's violin would call Sir back from the abyss.

Although visitors were not allowed, many people sent cards and letters. Brie read every single one out loud, trusting Sir could hear their messages of support. To keep his mind in the present, she also read the top stories from the news.

If researchers were right that patients in comas could hear, she knew Sir would want to be kept up to date with world news. She had opened up an article from the *LA Times* and paused, tears coming to her eyes. "Oh Sir, there is an article about you and the little girl you saved."

She choked up for a moment and then shared with him, "It says that churches all over LA. have picked up the plea of the Lucinda's mother and are praying for you." Brie put down her tablet and started to cry. "There are so many people who care about you, Sir. So many... It's time to wake up. We all need you to open your eyes."

She glanced at the monitor and frowned in disappointment. The rhythm of his heartbeat never changed. It didn't matter if his father's violin was playing or if she was holding his hand and telling him how much she loved him. Even when she snuck in their Wartenberg wheel and rolled it across his skin, it didn't evoke a reaction—nothing did.

She had watched Abby give Sir a sponge bath on several occasions, but this time when Abby came in, Brie asked if she could do it.

Abby gave it some thought before agreeing. "Certainly, Mrs. Davis. You've watched me, I'm sure you know the procedure."

She handed Brie the sponge and the tub of warm water. When she stepped aside to watch, Brie asked, "Do you mind if I do this alone?"

Understanding flooded Abby's face and she nodded, leaving quietly.

Brie looked at Sir. Most of the bandages had been removed, leaving him with the ventilator, his large cast, the braces on his feet, and a mess of tubes and numerous wires. It made bathing him more difficult, but she was not intimidated.

Sir looked peaceful lying there. The calm expression on his face made it appear as if he were just sleeping.

My handsome prince in need of a kiss to awaken you...

Brie leaned over and kissed his forehead, whispering,

"I know you're here with me. I want you to know how much I miss you."

She started at his feet, releasing the braces that helped keep them at a natural angle. She gently rubbed each foot with the wet cloth, making sure to give every toe individual care and attention. When she was done, she leaned down, her eyes locked on his face, as she lightly sucked and then bit down on his big toe. "That's right, husband. I'm going to make slow, delicious love to your body as I bathe you."

Brie smiled as she ran the sponge over the length of his left leg. Every inch of him was beautiful, from the sexy curve of his calf to the perfect shape of his kneecap. The dark hair that covered his skin only accented his masculinity. After cleaning around his right leg with the cast, she started with moisturizer, rubbing into his skin with the touch of a masseuse. She stimulated his muscles, pushing hard as her hands glided over his legs, inching ever closer to his upper thigh.

She looked at Sir again, grinning mischievously when she pulled his gown up and exposed his manly parts. "You *do* know where I'm headed, don't you?"

She massaged his thick thigh muscles, grazing the crease between his leg and groin, but never blatantly touching the area. She teased Sir the way he had so often teased her, and giggled lightly while she did it.

It gave her great satisfaction to see that his princely shaft hardened slightly without being touched. It proved to her that Sir was with her, feeling Brie's loving caress even if he could not respond to it.

She cleaned his pubic area gently and dried him, before bending down to lightly kiss that handsome cock.

Brie lowered the gown and then started on his arms, noting how strong and powerful they looked. She placed his hand against her cheek. "I've always admired your manly arms, Sir. They contain such strength and demand so much of my body, and yet…your touch can also be so very gentle." She placed his hand back down and purred. "I love these hands, Sir."

Brie carefully lowered his gown to run the sponge over his chest, appreciating his pecs, the dark hair, and that beautiful scar over his heart. Brie traced the small 't' with her finger, thinking back to that night they had both been branded.

"Condors forever."

She lifted her blouse and took his limp hand, turning her back toward him as she helped his fingers trace over her own brand. "Yours, Sir, until the end of time."

Brie swallowed back the lump in her throat as she put his hand back and straightened her blouse. She leaned down, stretching so she could kiss that brand on his chest. She washed his hands next, again taking time to focus on each finger, leaving no area untouched. Then she began the massage, letting his skin soak up the moisture as she stimulated the muscles underneath.

"Now for your handsome face…" she purred, rubbing her fingers over the overgrown stubble on his jaw. "As much as I love your facial hair, I need to give you a shave so you don't look quite so unruly, Sir."

She laughed lightly as she left to gather the materials needed from the nursing staff. When she returned, she used gentle hands to spread a thin layer of shaving cream on his jaw, doing her best to work around the tubes of the ventilator. Her hand was steady as she lifted off stubble with the razor, cleaning it before making another pass. Sir had allowed her to shave him a couple of times, and she'd found it extremely romantic.

She reminded him of that as she continued, sharing those memories as she sensually shaved him smooth. She leaned over to leave tiny kisses all over his newly shaved jaw. "So smooth and kissable..."

Brie had left his thick head of hair for last. The nurse had given her a shampoo that did not need to be rinsed out, so she put a dab in her palm and rubbed her hands together before she began massaging his scalp. "You are a very lucky man, Sir, getting the full body treatment from a beautiful woman. Some men pay big bucks for this."

She knew how delicious having one's hair washed was because it was something she'd cherished on the island. It pleased her to return the favor and lavish her attention on Sir now.

"Don't you love how it tingles, Master? That's what you do to me whenever you run your fingers through my hair. My whole body gets the chills. Isn't it heavenly?"

Even though he showed no change, Brie was positive he was enjoying himself. "I bet you're smiling right now. We need to get you off this ventilator so I can see it."

She leaned close to his ear and said, "I need you to fight through the fog that consumes you. Find me. Follow my voice, Thane... Come back to me." She kissed his cheek and went back to work.

After his entire scalp had received abundant attention, she got out the comb and styled his hair the way he normally wore it. Once she was done, Brie stood back and admired the man lying before her.

"You're one devilishly handsome man, Thane Davis."

Brie put all the bathing supplies on the counter and turned on the music before turning out the lights. Alonzo's haunting violin filled the darkened room as she returned to him, taking down the bedrail to join him.

She snuggled up beside Sir and closed her eyes. For a brief moment, Brie allowed herself to pretend they were back at the apartment, lying on their bed after a wondrous round of intense play—both of them basking in the glow of aftercare.

Master Anderson surprised Brie with an unexpected visit. Although she didn't want to leave Sir's side, she went out to meet him in the waiting room.

The Dom took one look at her and frowned.

Brie wanted to ease his worry. "Sir's doing better. His color is good, and the physical therapist is working hard on building his muscles so it won't be as difficult to move when he wakes."

"Brie…"

She was unnerved by his look of concern. "What is it, Master Anderson?"

"You look terrible. Have you been eating?"

"Of course I have. I make sure to eat three times a day," she stated defensively.

"*What* are you eating?"

She glanced at the floor before admitting, "Protein bars and nutritional shakes."

"And snacks from the vending machine, I'll wager."

Brie sighed, unable to protest his assertion.

"I'm disappointed in you, young Brie. That poor baby bump needs more than quick meals. You're compromising its health and we both know how anal Thane is about keeping you both healthy." He slapped his hand on his chest. "Damn, just looking at you breaks my heart."

"I'm fine," she insisted. "Everything's fine."

"Everything is definitely *not* fine. Thane is still in a coma and his wife is killing herself trying to bring him back. He would not appreciate you sacrificing the health of your baby bump in the process."

Brie took offense and retorted angrily, "I *will* not leave Sir's side before he wakes. I can't and I won't!" She felt the rush of blood to her head and turned away from him before she lost her balance.

"Sit down," he commanded, guiding her to a seat before announcing, "I'll be right back."

He returned a short time later with a bowl of chicken noodle soup from the cafeteria and a banana. "It's the best I could do on short notice."

She reluctantly took the banana from him, although she secretly appreciated his effort. Under Master Anderson's watchful eyes, she unpeeled it and began to nibble on the soft fruit.

"I've heard from the nurses that you rarely leave here, Brie."

"The doctor gave me permission to stay."

"But it's obvious you aren't getting enough sleep. With the staff coming in at all hours of the night to check his vitals, it's no wonder you look like hell."

"I've adjusted to their schedules," she replied earnestly, needing him to understand. "The truth is I would get much less sleep if I went back to our empty apartment."

He huffed, looking unconvinced. "As Thane's friend, I can't stand idly by and watch you waste away like this. He would never forgive me. Hell, I wouldn't be able to forgive myself."

"I'm doing fine."

"I will bend you over and spank you if you say that again," he growled. "I bet he thinks you deserve one and wouldn't have an issue if I were to deliver it."

Brie scooted away from him, unsure if he would really go through with such a thing.

"I'll make sure to eat more from now on. I promised Captain I would eat three times a day and I have kept that promise. If I tell you I will eat better, you can trust I will."

Master Anderson's lips were pressed in a straight line, letting her know he was not happy with that arrangement.

She snarled in response to his silence. "I'm not going home to that empty apartment, damn it. Nothing you say is going to make me do that."

He raised an eyebrow, a smile slowly curling his lips.

"Is that a challenge, young Brie?"

"It's a fact."

"You are a feisty one, I'll give you that." He grabbed her in a bear hug, refusing to let go.

His embrace seemed to free her pent-up emotions, and she finally admitted as she sniffled, "Nothing's changed, Master Anderson. I've tried everything I can think of, but he hasn't opened his eyes. He's..." She paused for a moment, her voice quavering when she admitted, "He's just like his mother."

Brie broke down in a torrent of tears as the hopelessness of the situation hit her head-on.

"No," Master Anderson said gruffly, tightening his embrace.

"I've failed him," she mumbled against his chest.

"The only thing you've failed at is taking care of yourself." He tilted her head up. "Thane *will* wake, but I guarantee you he'll kill me if he sees you looking like this."

Brie smiled reluctantly, but then the floodgates opened, and for the first time since finding Sir alive but unconscious Brie let it all out—the fear, the anger, the helplessness, and the deep feeling of loss. It was ugly and loud, but she could not stop the pent-up emotions that demanded release.

By the time the flood finally subsided, Master Anderson's shirt was thoroughly soaked. She patted the wet shirt, her eyes puffy and painful, and her nose still running. "I'm sorry."

He only laughed. "Not a problem."

Ripping off his shirt, he lay it on a chair to dry and

grabbed the tissue box for her. "Tears dry up, but bottled emotions fester. Now blow."

She smiled sadly as she took the Kleenex he offered and dutifully blew into it. Brie felt completely exhausted after that burst of emotion, to the point that she just wanted to curl up on the floor and go to sleep.

Master Anderson took her numerous used tissues and stood up to toss them in the garbage. He was an impressive sight. One of the nurses walking by gasped audibly when she saw him bare-chested.

He chuckled as he explained to her the reason for his state of undress. "My shirt was sacrificed for the damsel in distress," he said, pointing to Brie.

"Aww..." the nurse cooed sweetly, turning to Brie and suddenly realizing by her red-rimmed eyes and blotchy face that Brie was not doing well. "It's good you have support, Mrs. Davis."

Brie noticed the nurse kept glancing at Master Anderson's chest even as she tried to console Brie. Before the nurse left, she asked him, "Would you like me to have that dried for you?"

He bestowed her with a melt worthy grin as he handed over the shirt, tipping an imaginary hat. "Much obliged, miss."

The nurse blushed as she took the sopping wet clothing, a shy smile on her lips. Before she left, however, she turned back to Brie. "Don't lose hope, Mrs. Davis. He's stable."

Brie nodded in acknowledgement, but when the nurse was gone she added, "Stable, but nothing has changed."

"You're wrong there, young Brie," Master Anderson answered. "Something significant has happened here."

She gave him a dubious look. "What?"

"I'm going to be watching over you until he wakes."

Brie was touched by the offer, but felt she needed to be honest. "I can't drive all the way from your home to the hospital every day. It's too far."

"I know this, young Brie. That's why I'll be staying with you—along with Cayenne, of course. You know, the little spitfire you gifted me."

Brie smiled at the mention of the orange tabby.

He pointed his finger at her. "See? I already have you smiling. In a few days' time, under my care, you should be well fed and rested." When she opened her mouth to protest, he stopped her. "No, you do not have a say in this. I refuse to suffer the wrath of Thane to placate your ego."

The sudden urge to curl up on the floor returned when she tried to stand up and she swayed slightly.

"See? You're only helping my case. Now you go back to your husband and explain to him that you will be back bright and early tomorrow."

It actually hurt Brie's heart, the thought of leaving Sir alone in the cold hospital room. She would have cried, but her tears were all dried up. She walked back into Sir's room, dreading having to tell him she was leaving his side.

In a hoarse whisper she explained, "I have to leave tonight, Sir. Master Anderson's orders. But I will be back early tomorrow. Know that I will always come back to you." She leaned over and kissed his unresponsive lips.

Master Anderson stood waiting for her, taking her purse and offering his other arm to her. She smiled sadly as she took it and headed toward the elevator.

"What about your shirt?" she protested, stopping in the middle of the hallway.

Master Anderson shrugged, grinning when he answered, "I'll get it tomorrow. I'm sure the nursing staff won't mind."

Brie noted the lustful glances in Master Anderson's direction from passersby as the two stood waiting for the elevator. It reminded her of his gardening days and the enjoyment he found in showing off his naked chest to the ladies of his neighborhood.

Some people never changed… and Brie was glad for it.

The first thing Master Anderson did when they entered the apartment was to check through the refrigerator and cupboards.

"What the heck is this?" he growled in disgust, holding up a nutritional supplement drink. "You have cases and cases of this crap. Isn't that for *old* people?"

She grabbed the can from him and said defensively, "It's a quick and nutritious drink. Leave me alone."

"If you give birth to an old man, I'll know why."

"Stop it!" she cried, giggling despite her irritation.

He picked up two giant boxes of soda crackers. "And these?" he asked accusingly.

"Sometimes my tummy gets upset and they are the only thing I can stomach."

Master Anderson got down on his knees and spoke to her stomach. "Hey baby bump, I'm sorry. I had no idea your mommy was abusing you."

Brie pushed him away, trying not to smile. "I take my prenatal vitamins every day, and I never skip a meal. I assure you there is no abuse going on."

"We need some real food in this house! While you get my bed ready, I'll head to the store after I pick up Cayenne, of course, and snag myself a new shirt."

"Would you like me to get you one of Sir's?"

"There's no way I could fit into one of his tiny ass shirts," he said, flexing his beefy arms.

She laughed. "I'll be sure to tell him you said that." Then she added wistfully, "It *will* be nice to have some life in this place." Her smile soon disappeared, however, as unwanted tears welled up in her eyes. "God, I miss him."

Master Anderson wrapped her in his husky embrace. "I know you miss him, but no crying. I'm no good with tears." His hug was comforting until he started to tickle her.

Brie burst out in giggles as she struggled to get out of his vise-like embrace. "Go get that kitten already, and leave me be," she scolded.

When he let her go, she asked hesitantly, "Master Anderson, do you mind if I sleep with her tonight?"

He answered in a somber tone, "Not at all. I'm sure she would prefurrrr that."

Brie shook her head as she shooed him out the door,

thinking it was very possible he'd spent a little *too* much time with Lea in Denver.

Knowing the apartment wouldn't be empty for long gave Brie renewed energy and she quickly made up the bed for Master Anderson before heading out for a quick trip to the grocery store around the corner. Luckily, not only did they carry cat litter, but she also found a feathery cat toy hanging on a stick.

As a gift for Master Anderson, Brie bought a cheap whoopee cushion from the kiddie section and laughed to herself as she waited in line, knowing exactly where she'd put it.

Brie was filling a large plastic container with cat litter when she heard Master Anderson knock on the door. She ran up throwing the door open to him, begging to hold Cayenne.

However, when she spied the animal she was heartbroken. "Has it really been that long? She isn't a tiny kitten anymore," Brie cried forlornly.

"No, she is a young lady now," Master Anderson stated, handing the orange furball over.

To Brie's delight, Cayenne snuggled against her chest and started purring. It was just what her soul needed. She looked up at Master Anderson and mouthed the words, "Thank you."

He nodded. "Isn't it nice when the gift you give someone turns out to be a gift for yourself?"

She giggled when Cayenne rubbed her furry cheek again Brie's chin. "I really just wanted you to break out of your loneliness when I gave her to you."

"Hmm…maybe that is Cayenne's role for you as

well."

Brie stared at the cat with a bemused expression. "Wouldn't that be a strange twist of fate?"

"While you two get reacquainted, I'll make my famous tomato bisque so it can start simmering. I'm determined to make that baby bump happy."

"My little one won't be happy until her daddy is well again."

"Ah, but you forget the legendary power of my soup."

Brie laughed. "I'll concede your soup does have supernatural powers."

"So while I prepare it settle down on the couch. Watch yourself a girlie movie and veg out."

She couldn't stomach the thought of watching TV, since that was what she'd been doing the night of the crash. Instead, Brie picked up the cat toy and headed toward the sofa. She let the feathered bird drag along the ground, knowing it would be an irresistible temptation for Cayenne.

The cat crouched down, wiggling her hind end as she prepared to attack the moving object. Brie let out an involuntary squeak when the attack came.

Cayenne was a ferocious beast!

She jumped on the feather creature and curled herself around it, clawing the poor thing with her powerful hind legs. It didn't take long until Brie pronounced the toy dead. She held up the lone feather still attached to the string and looked at Master Anderson, pouting. "Your cat killed my toy."

He nodded proudly. "Best huntress I know."

Brie dangled the feather above Cayenne, barely fast enough to jerk it up before the tabby leaped into the air to end the toy's misery.

"I would hate to be a bird around her," Brie muttered.

"No chick better mess with my Cayenne."

Brie sat down on the couch, gingerly laying what was left of the bird on the coffee table. The moment Brie put the stick down, it was if a switch had suddenly been flipped inside Cayenne. The master huntress morphed back into a cuddly feline, jumping on Brie to curl up on her lap. When she started to purr, Brie bit her lip at the adorableness of it.

"She's just too darn cute."

Master Anderson chuckled from the kitchen. "Yes, she's the best companion a man could ask for."

"Except for a devoted submissive, of course."

"Trust me, Cayenne is far less complicated."

Brie tsked, shaking her head in disagreement. "But I didn't get you Cayenne so you could continue living a solitary life."

Master Anderson came out of the kitchen with two grilled cheese sandwiches. Cayenne launched herself off of Brie and enthusiastically brushed her body against her master, weaving in and out of his legs. He held the plates above his head and used them for balance as he successfully avoided tripping over the affectionate feline.

He shrugged as he handed a plate to Brie. "You know, there's nothing wrong with being alone, Mrs. Davis."

Brie looked up at him frowning slightly as she took

it. "No, there isn't, unless you have a soulmate waiting for you somewhere."

Master Anderson cleared his throat as if the suggestion made him uncomfortable. "Hmm…" He sat down beside her and a long, muffled farting noise escaped from under the sofa cushion.

Brie started to giggle. "Really, Master Anderson, I'm trying to eat."

He threw his head back and let out a full-on belly laugh. Afterward he wiped his eyes and exclaimed, "Oh hell…I needed that."

Once his laughter subsided, Cayenne jumped up onto Master Anderson's lap, extremely interested in the sandwich on his plate. He smiled at Brie, explaining, "Cayenne has a thing for my cooking. She puts her nose up whenever I try feeding her traditional cat food."

Brie picked up a piece of her sandwich and watched with satisfaction as cheese oozed from it. She purred in pleasure. "Nothing like a grilled cheese sandwich."

"Melty goodness for the soul," Master Anderson agreed, taking a bite of his before breaking off a piece for Cayenne. The cat licked his offering several times before gracefully taking it from his hand.

"I would give you and baby bump the soup, but it needs to simmer a while so the flavors can be fully realized."

"I can't wait to meet you here for dinner tomorrow, Master Anderson. It's been a while since I had anyone waiting for me at home."

He put his muscular arm around her shoulder. "I'm sure, but all that's changed now." He frowned at her reproachfully. "You know that you only needed to reach out and I would have been here in a heartbeat. Heck, any of us would."

Brie shrugged. "I didn't think I needed it. My sole focus this whole time—the only thing I care about—is seeing Sir open his eyes. Even now, I'm panicking a little because he might wake up and I won't be there."

"Thane doesn't need you to live at the hospital twenty-four seven, young Brie."

"It's not what he needs, it's about what I need. I have to be there when Sir awakens."

"And you will be—looking all rosy-cheeked and giddy, the picture of health. Then he will turn to me and say, 'Well done, Brad. Way to take care of my girl while I was out for the count.'"

Brie giggled. "That will not be the first thing out of his mouth."

He held out his hand. "Wanna bet?"

"Ten bucks."

"Fine, show me yours and I will show you mine." Brie dug a ten dollar bill out of her purse and placed it on the table. He whipped out his wallet and put down a twenty, taking her ten. "Hah, I was needing a ten."

Master Anderson then picked up the twenty and put it on Sir's desk. "When it comes time to collect on the bet, we can explain it to Thane."

"Good, because I've already decided what to buy with it," Brie informed him.

"What?"

Brie grinned to herself, imagining numerous whoopee cushions to hide all over his new home. "My secret."

Cayenne moved back to Brie and settled on her stomach, closing her eyes with a look of contentment. Brie started to pet her, grateful for the physical connection.

"Looks like she's settling in just fine. I'll go finish up in the kitchen while the two of you females bond."

Brie laid her head back against the arm of the couch, taking Cayenne's example and closing her own eyes. It was nice to hear the sound of dishes clinking as the aroma of cooking food wafted from the kitchen.

It was…normal.

And normal felt so incredibly good to Brie right now.

Hope

B rie woke up early, before the sun had even risen, and quietly dressed. Cayenne was not happy with the earliness of the hour and moved onto Brie's pillow to snuggle back down. Brie couldn't blame the cat, and petted her on the head before she left.

"Sleep well, little huntress."

Brie snuck past the guest room, dutifully getting one of her nutrition drinks and a protein bar from the pantry. When she opened the pantry door, however, she found a note.

I made you a breakfast burrito chock full of healthy veggies with cheese and eggs for protein, so put down those poor excuses for nutrition and take it instead. You'll find a lunch bag in the fridge with your name clearly printed on it.

Brie smiled as she opened up the refrigerator and saw an insulated lunch bag with "Brie and Baby Bump" written on it in permanent marker. She grabbed it out of the fridge and snuck a peek inside. Not only was there a foil-wrapped burrito, but a big container of his soup, a spoon, and plenty of fruit and raw vegetables—plus a few of her soda crackers.

She looked down the hall, deeply touched by his thoughtfulness.

Brie entered Sir's room with a sense of real hope. It was amazing what a good night's sleep and a home-cooked meal could do for a person.

"I'm back, Sir!" she exclaimed, brushing back his hair back to give Sir a kiss on the forehead. "I hope you had a good night's rest. I know I did."

Brie went on to tell him everything that had happened with Master Anderson: from playing with Cayenne, the silly bet, the good food, to the fun of the whoopie cushion. She laughed out loud just talking about it.

As was her new habit, Brie kept stealing glances at his heart monitor, hoping to see a change in his breathing or heartbeat, but it remained as constant and unchanging as ever. Still, she couldn't contain the optimism she felt as she took out her burrito and left him for a short time to heat it up.

When she returned, Brie took a big bite and purred. "Doesn't that smell delicious, Sir?" She took another, making a genuine sound of pleasure. "Oh my, this is even better than the first bite. Master Anderson is an incredible cook!"

Brie had the brilliant idea of wafting it up to his nose and for the first time, there was a reaction on his monitor—a slight increase of his heartbeat. Proof positive that he was there and that he was aware enough to smell the food. Brie continued to share the smell of it as she wolfed down the burrito, realizing she'd forgotten the satisfaction of feeling full.

She sighed in contentment when she was done, patting her bloated belly. "I bet you are satisfied too, little one." Brie balled up the foil and aimed it at the wastepaper basket. It rolled against the rim before falling in.

"Score!"

She smiled at Sir. "Just like old times."

Brie was inspired now, certain that if she could find the right combination of stimuli he would come back to her.

She brought her fantasy journal the next day. "Do you remember when you told me to write this, Sir? You didn't get the chance to read it, so I thought I would read it out loud to you now."

She caressed the page before beginning. "I was inspired by our Fiji experience."

Brie took a deep breath, wanting to convey the story in the same spirit it was written, ignoring all the tubes, monitors, and the sterile environment of the hospital.

"I am the proud daughter of my father, Semi—the leader of the isle. Our island is the jewel of the sea. With lush vegetation, abundant sea life, fresh water, and long white beaches, it is the envy of all of our neighbors. But what makes our island unique are the rocks that are found here.

We are known as the warrior artists, esteemed for our unique stone carvings and intricate neck ornaments. Word of our work has traveled far, and we are often approached for trade. It benefits us to trade, because it allows my father to keep the peace while maintaining our prominence among the other islands. Although we are a peaceful people, throughout history, bloodshed has stained our isle. We are not savages, but we will fight fearlessly to keep what we have.

I would die to protect my isle and its people…

I am headed back to speak with my father after finding an unusual blue stone. It glitters in the sun, and I trust my father will be able to tell me what it is. I'm already envisioning the shape of a dolphin, my fingers itching to work on it.

My mind is distracted as I top the crest of the hill that overlooks my home. To my horror I see strangers surrounding the village and hear the terrified cries of my family and friends as they are herded to the center.

I instantly drop to the ground, hoping I have not been spotted. I cannot fathom how my father was taken by surprise, but I quickly begin formulating a plan of rescue as I watch the foreigners.

A cold chill envelops me when I realize they are not of this world. Their skin is a ghostly white, not like the deep brown of ours, and they speak with strange utterances. I caress the knife by my side, grateful for its protection. My father always insisted I carry a weapon at all times. Now I understand his vigilance.

I creep a little closer, wanting to observe these otherworldly beings before I make my move. I know that one must understand the enemy to defeat them.

I crouch low and observe the ghost who appears to be the leader. As horrified as I am by his appearance, I am fascinated by the color of his hair. It reminds me of the color of our sand.

My heart beats faster as he separates from the group and heads up the hill toward me. I flatten myself to the ground.

His eyes…they match the blue stone I hold in my hand.

Is it a sign?

I wonder if I am meant to slay him. Normally, such a kill is reserved for the chieftain, but am I not the daughter of one?

I look up briefly at the clouds and silently sing my death song to the ancestors.

I will kill him, but understand there is no way I can survive the onslaught of the foreigners. The chaos caused by the death of their leader and myself will allow my people to overcome their captors.

It is an honor that I have been chosen by the gods for this.

I let go of the rock as I tense for the attack, the blade gripped tightly in my other hand. I attack before he even sees me coming, but he is strong and agile, avoiding the worst of my blade. I only leave a minor wound.

However, I have been trained to fight and return with a swift side kick that causes him to lose his balance. Before he can recover I am on top of him, my knife raised and my path clear.

But I hesitate for the briefest of moments when I gaze into his strange eyes. That hesitation costs me the kill. He rolls his body over, taking me with him and I find myself crushed by his weight. I struggle for all I am worth, but know I am about to die without victory.

The ghost man chuckles to himself. It infuriates me, to be laughed at and I break one hand free, reaching between his legs to squeeze the life out of his manhood. He freezes for a moment and that is all I need to push him off.

There will be no hesitation this time.

I raise the blade, ready to drive it into his ghostly heart—but I am never given the chance. Rough hands grab me from behind as the knife is wrestled out of my grip. It falls to the ground along with any chance of victory.

The men are not gentle when they pull my arms back, and I grimace from the pain but refuse to cry out. Instead, I hold my chin up, ready to meet my ancestors with the dignity of a warrior.

One of the men presses his blade against my neck, but the ghost man speaks and the sharp blade is removed. He moves in closer to stare at me as if I disturb him as much he unsettles me. I close my eyes, unnerved by those blue orbs and silently curse at the rock on the ground.

I thought it foretold my victory, but its true purpose was to announce my doom.

The honor of death is denied me, and I am further humiliated when his men drag me through the village. I bow my head in shame, having failed in my duty. I cannot look my father in the eye as they parade me past.

I have betrayed my people by failing to protect them.

They forced me towards the strange vessel they came in. It is truly horrifying in its size and structure. Surely this ship will return to the bowels of Mother Earth and I will become like these ghost men.

I begin biting, clawing and writhing, trying to break myself free from their clutches, but four more appear to subdue me. I am helpless as they carry me onto the dreaded craft.

The size of it is daunting. I understand that any being that could build such a thing intends to conquer the seas. I look back to my isle, knowing my people are lost. They do not deserve what these ghost men will do.

The sweaty, foul-smelling men drag me down below to a dark room and tie me to a post there. One tries to touch my chest but I gnash my teeth and he barely avoids the bite. The other men laugh, smacking his back as they exit the room.

I glance around, the only light coming from two small round windows. I spy a weapon displayed on a wall and smile. How stupid are these ghost men?

With determination, I begin rubbing the rope against the pole, unmindful of how it cuts into my skin. My only goal is to escape with their prized weapon.

The rope is thick and my progress is slow, but the heat of my bindings lets me know my efforts are working. I hear heavy footsteps and instantly stop, bowing my head to communicate my defeat.

The door opens and I hold my breath as he approaches. I know it is the blue-eyed ghost; his smell permeates the room. Whereas the other men's odor is disgusting, his is not, and that frightens me.

He says something, but I do not move.

To my disappointment, he reaches around to feel the ropes that bind me and laughs. He forces my chin up with a strong grip and looks me in the eye. Again he speaks. I cannot understand his words, but the tone of his voice is passionate—not angry.

He lets go of my chin and takes a seat on a bed in the corner. He lays back casually and dares to smirk at me.

Anger rises up like fire inside my belly. I know the danger he represents and will not be made to feel like a fool by his dismissive manner. I snarl in response.

He nods his head, seeming to enjoy my fury which only infuriates me more.

The ghost man starts talking again in a smooth tone as he stands up and starts to remove his protective clothing. My eyes are transfixed, like a small animal who is about to be snuffed out by its predator but is unable to move. I watch as he removes his shirt and exposes his chest to me.

My eyes widen. Although his skin is as ghostly pale as the face, it is covered in the same sand-colored hair—like an animal. I swallow. He is truly not of this world…

My gaze is riveted on his naked chest as he slowly approaches me. Chills take over when I feel his touch on my cheek and he leans down to kiss me. The connection is so foreign it terrifies me, but I am powerless as my body instinctually responds to the kiss.

The ghost man breaks away with a knowing smile. He puts his hand to his chest and utters the sound, "James." He then points to me.

I close my lips tight.

"James," he repeats in a commanding tone.

I try to say the strange name, but my mouth is not used to uttering such sounds.

He nods his approval at my attempt, leaning in for another kiss. My heart races when our mouths connect. I am certain now he has put a spell on me.

His tongue parts my lips, and this time I am the one to pull away, truly frightened by the strange kiss.

The ghost man chuckles, caressing my cheek again. He has a dark magic that soothes my soul.

I stare at him like a frightened animal when he kisses me again, tasting me with his tongue as he robs me of all my defenses.

My body is mesmerized by his commanding presence, and I do not move when he pulls out his knife. He reaches behind me, freeing me from the rope. Then he pulls me to the bed, pushing me onto it with his own body weight.

The heft of it crushes my chest and I can barely breathe as he grabs my head with both hands and kisses me again, thrusting his tongue into my mouth more aggressively.

I do not offer resistance, allowing his exploration. I am aroused by it. This stranger—this ghost of a man—will take me to his dark depths, and I find myself desperate to follow.

I feel him lift up the material of my clothing with one hand while he continues to kiss me deeply. I should fight, but I want what he is demanding of me.

His hands explore my body while his tongue plunders my mouth. I am lost in his sensual caresses and close my eyes so that I can only feel and not think about what is happening.

But he pulls away and stands up. I open my eyes, holding my breath as I watch him remove the rest of his clothing. His hairiness extends from his chest to his legs, reminding me that he is other-worldly.

His pale manhood is hard and ready. The fear sets in again…

He speaks to me in soothing tones as he begins to undress me. I feel like an insect caught in a spider web, powerless to stop its impending doom.

The contrast of his pale skin against the dark brown of mine is captivating. We should not mate, it is wrong, and yet everything in me wants to know his ghostly touch. To feel his possession as he mounts me.

I lay naked before him as he gazes over my body shamelessly. Spreading my legs, he positions himself between my thighs. I turn away, not wanting to witness my descent into depravity, but he turns my head back making it clear I'm to watch.

His thick white member pushes into my darkness. For a moment I cannot breathe, as his fullness takes over my reality.

I cry out as he takes hold of my hips and pushes in farther. He grabs my wrists and begins to thrust. Chills take over my body, making my nipples hard and tight.

The ghost is inside me.

I stare up into his blue eyes, surrendering my soul to him—my descent complete.

Brie closed the journal and glanced at the monitor. No change.

She stood up and leaned over to kiss Sir on the lips whispering lovingly, "Wake up, my ghost."

Brie had just turned on Alonzo's touching solo, the one Sir often made love to her by. She was lost in her memories when she heard one of the nurses come into the room. Being used to the constant interruptions, Brie did not even bother to open her eyes.

"Hello, Brianna."

Brie's heart skipped a beat, recognizing the unwelcomed voice. She opened her eyes to see Lilly standing before her.

"Why are you here?" Brie demanded.

"I'm family."

Brie stood up and made her way over to Sir, staring at Lilly was if she were a snake that might strike at any second. "Sir ordered you never to come around us again."

Lilly smiled as she nonchalantly took off the wrap she wore, exposing a distinctly pregnant belly. Brie couldn't breathe as she watched Lilly caress it. "I hear congratulations are in order, Mrs. Davis. It appears both you and I will be having a child of Thane's."

Brie began trembling all over. "I don't believe you."

Lilly pointed to her stomach and looked at her incredulously. "The proof's right in front of your face. You and I both know what happened that night in China."

Brie gripped the bed frame, steadying herself. Lilly looked to be the right number of months along, enough for her story to be true. Brie licked her lips, suddenly feeling light-headed.

"I didn't come here for myself, Brianna. I'm here to protect the rights of my child—Thane's child. The honorable thing for you to do is to accept the financial responsibility you owe this baby."

Brie looked down at Sir, lying there so peaceful and innocent. He'd claimed Lilly's accusations were lies and she had believed him, but seeing Lilly now with a rounded belly…

"I still don't believe you."

Lilly laughed condescendingly. "Well, I've had a paternity test done. There is no doubt who the father is."

Brie felt the ground begin to shift beneath her feet.

"I only expect half."

"Half of what?"

"Half of whatever he leaves you in the will."

Brie growled, "Thane's not dead!"

Lilly glanced at her half-brother dismissively. "He will be as soon as you turn off the ventilator. Serves him right for what he did to my mother—and me."

"If you've come for money, you're in for a shock. Sir hasn't awakened, and until he does and can defend himself personally, you won't see anything from his estate."

Lilly's angry laughter filled the room. "I'm sure the courts will have a different opinion, Mrs. Davis. And then there's the court of public opinion. How will people feel about your husband after I share what he's done? Do you think your next film will even see the light of day when they discover the monster your *Master* truly is?"

Lilly's tone and actions echoed of Ruth's cruelty. The fact she looked so similar to the dead woman was absolutely terrifying. It was as if the Beast had never died, risen from the ashes through her daughter to further torment them.

Even with the evidence before her, something felt off about Lilly's accusation. Why hadn't she pressed formal charges? Why was she willing to break a restraining order to get Brie alone?

"It feels to me that you are using the child as a pawn," Brie accused.

Lilly became livid, hissing in rage. "This is the baby *he* created. How can you even defend such a man?"

"Thane wouldn't—"

"But he did," she howled in disgust. "And I have living proof."

The floor seemed to sway more violently. Brie gripped the bed tighter to steady herself.

Lilly moved up to the other side of Sir and leaned down. "I'm back, Thane. What you did is unforgivable, and something you will pay dearly for."

Brie saw his heartbeat increase briefly, an outward sign he was aware of Lilly's presence.

"You need to leave now. I'm certain Sir has a restraining order against you."

Lilly looked at her in disbelief. "Are you threatening me after what he's done?"

"You're not allowed to be anywhere near either of us," Brie stated, not backing down.

Lilly looked Brie dead in the eye. "I'm willing to leave your life for good if you give me half of the estate." Her expression became deadly when she added, "However, should you choose *not* to support this child, I will go to the press first, and the courts next. Make no mistake about that, Mrs. Davis."

Brie was sickened by the fact Lilly planned to destroy Sir's reputation just as her mother had destroyed Alonzo's all those years ago, but Brie would not allow that to happen again!

"When you say you plan to go the press first it proves to me your motives are not to benefit the child."

Lilly spat. "My *only* concern is for this baby. If you two get damaged by the cross-fire, what the fuck do I care? Your silence all these months only proves you're covering up for a man who should be rotting in jail for his crimes—and you know it."

Brie noticed another spike in his heart rate. "You need to leave. Now!"

"I give you two weeks to buy my silence—after that

it's a free-for-all. It's the exact same offer I made Thane."

"What are you talking about?"

"He knows about the baby, but apparently he didn't tell you. Interesting... Why do you think that is, Mrs. Davis?"

Brie was rattled by the question but shot back, "Why would you offer your silence to the man who allegedly assaulted you?"

Lilly shrugged. "If I had a choice, I would prefer my child not live with the knowledge of what happened." She rubbed her stomach for dramatic effect. "So, let me raise the child as an innocent, giving the boy the best care Thane can afford."

When Lilly saw the shocked look on Brie face, she smiled. "Oh yes, it's a boy." She stared pointedly at Brie's flat stomach. "Let's hope you don't have a miscarriage. It'd be a shame considering Thane's condition now."

She looked down at him lying still in the bed. "Who knows? I may end up being the only one to carry on his bloodline. How grossly ironic would that be?"

"Get out!"

Lilly was in no hurry as she made her way to the door. "Two weeks, Mrs. Davis. Enough time to get your finances in order to pay me. Otherwise, the world will know the truth *and* I will still get the money..." Lilly pointed her finger at Brie. "Don't be an idiot."

After Lilly's exit, Brie found she could not even look at Sir. She distinctly remembered the mysterious letter, the one he had proceeded to ripped up into tiny pieces after reading it. Was that why Sir had acted so strangely? Had he been trying cover up the truth from her?

When Abby came through the door, Brie looked up at her helplessly before her knees buckled and everything went black.

Brie woke with a start and found herself staring into the dreamy green eyes of Master Anderson.

"Are you okay, young Brie?"

She nodded automatically until the memories of what happened flooded in. Brie began shaking her head, as tears welled up in her eyes.

"I heard Thane's half-sister paid a visit," he stated calmly.

Brie nodded but said no more, not wanting Master Anderson to know the circumstances behind the visit.

"I called Thane's attorney and he's on it."

She looked at him dubiously. "Do you know why she came to the hospital?"

"I do. Thane told me about the incident in China. She's obviously come back to stir up trouble while he is lying unconscious. A despicable act from a cowardly woman."

Brie still wasn't sure if he knew about the pregnancy. "What did Mr. Thompson tell you when you spoke with him?"

"He suggested you call the police if she should attempt to contact you again. I have already informed the hospital staff that there is a restraining order against her."

Skirting the issue, she asked, "Did you see her, Master Anderson?"

"No, she had left by the time I arrived. Which is lucky for her. I don't react kindly to anyone who would dare to harass you at a time like this."

"Thank you, Master Anderson," she whispered.

He gazed at Brie for several moments before commenting. "You still seemed troubled. What exactly did she say to you?"

Brie swallowed hard. "I think I should talk to Sir's lawyer."

Master Anderson tilted his head, trying to figure her out. "You can tell me anything, young Brie. I would never break that confidence."

"No," she said, feeling nauseous. "I can't."

"What has she done?" he demanded.

Brie looked him in the eyes. "Please, Master Anderson. Take me to see Mr. Thompson."

"Now?"

"Yes."

"You just fainted. The only place you're headed is home."

She started to get up against his wishes, stating, "If you won't take me I will call a cab. I *need* to see him in person as soon as possible."

"Damn it! What is it you aren't telling me?" he asked sternly.

Brie said nothing as she started for the door.

"Are you going to say good-bye to Thane before we

go?"

"No," Brie answered, relieved to hear that he was planning to take her.

Master Anderson grabbed her shoulders and turned her around forcibly to face him. "Holy hell, what has that witch done to you?"

Brie dropped her gaze, fighting back the tears unsuccessfully.

"I will strangle that woman to within an inch of her life when I see her!"

She looked up at him and begged earnestly, "Don't go anywhere near Lilly, please."

"You do realize it's my duty to protect you."

"If you care about Sir, you will heed my warning."

Master Anderson growled in frustration.

"Promise me."

He snarled, "This is not like you—this is beneath you."

Brie's voice was grave when she warned, "Master Anderson, Lilly has the power to change the course of our lives. Any direct contact might set off a chain of events that we won't recover from."

Still not convinced, he snarled under his breath. "I sincerely hope his lawyer can talk some sense into you. I can't fathom what has you running so scared."

It was a great relief once Brie was alone in the conference room with Mr. Thompson. She felt certain Sir would have confided in him after receiving news of the pregnancy, so there was no reason to hold anything back. "As you already know, Lilly came to the hospital today. You are also probably aware that Lilly is claiming that she carries Thane's child."

"He did contact me about the issue. What exactly did she relay to you at the hospital?"

"She told me she has had a genetic test done which proves the baby is his."

Mr. Thompson began scribbling on a notepad as she spoke. "Go on…"

"She wants half of his money to raise the child." He did not bat an eye at the amount, which led Brie to ask, "She told me she gave Sir the same offer. To take half of his estate in exchange for her silence. Is that true?"

Mr. Thompson put down his pen and stated frankly, "Yes, Mr. Davis was given a threat of blackmail stating those exact terms."

"Why didn't he tell me?" Brie demanded.

"He and I both believe the allegations are false. There was no need to concern you, unless it's proven otherwise."

"I hate to be the one to inform you, Mr. Thompson, but she *is* pregnant. Far enough along to make her story plausible."

"Are you saying you believe Mr. Davis is the father of the child?"

"I…" Brie stammered. "I don't know what I believe anymore."

"Did Mr. Davis give you any cause to believe he assaulted her that night?"

"No, other than the fact he became so inebriated that he was suffering from an extreme headache the next morning and wasn't himself. He even admitted that he couldn't remember anything about that night."

"Do you remember any scratch marks or bruises on his body that might indicate a struggle?"

"Not that I recall."

"So as far as the law is concerned there is no hard evidence to validate her claims."

"Except for the genetic test," she reminded him harshly.

"That is also hearsay at this point. Until I have documented proof from a trusted source, I will not consider it."

Brie let out a sigh of relief, grasping desperately onto the hope that it might not be Thane's child. The fact was Brie had never forgotten the haunted look in Lilly's eyes when she'd made her accusations while in China. Something terrible *had* happened to the woman, Brie was convinced of that.

"Lilly told me that if I do not give her the money within two weeks, she will go to the press and the legal system to expose the truth."

"It sounds like extortion."

"But here's the real issue, the one I can't ignore, Mr. Thompson. Even if she is lying, and this is not Sir's child, when Lilly tells the press, his reputation will be forever suspect—just like his father's. Just the simple allegation itself will be enough to destroy him, especially if he cannot defend himself."

Mr. Thompson nodded. "I understand your concern

and it is a valid one. I have to assume she will attempt to contact you again. I advise you to call the authorities if she tries to corner you in public. I'd prefer she contact you by phone so we can record any conversations you have to use as evidence against her."

Brie paused before asking her deepest fear. "But what if it is Sir's child?"

"Rest assured, I am prepared to cross that bridge if we must."

She was brutally honest with him. "My support for my husband may change depending on the test results."

He sighed deeply, interlacing his fingers together. "I can understand, Mrs. Davis, but you and I *must* proceed under the assumption her accusations are false and Mr. Davis is innocent."

Brie looked out the conference room window, her emotions a tangled mess of loyalty and mistrust. "That may be hard for me to do."

"I'm sure I don't need to warn you to keep the details of this to yourself."

She huffed. "I'm very aware of that, Mr. Thompson. This secret has the potential to tear down everything Sir has built."

Including my heart... she added silently.

Brie left Mr. Thompson feeling more in control. Although she still had to face Lilly and her claims against Sir, at least she had someone on her side who was as determined as she was to protect Sir's reputation until the truth could be sifted out.

"Did the meeting go well?" Master Anderson asked when he saw her emerge from the conference room.

"As well as possible," she answered sadly.

"Will you tell me what's going on?"

"No, under the advisement of my lawyer."

He shook his head in disbelief. "She's legitimately got you running scared."

"As Sir's friend, I need you not to engage Lilly in any way."

"I give you my word, but I'd prefer to know why."

She wrapped her arms around Master Anderson and pressed her head against his hard chest. "I wish I could tell you, if only for the words of wisdom and comfort you could provide."

He grasped her shoulders and pull away to look into her eyes. "Never question Thane's integrity. He is one of the most honorable men I know."

"I agree…"

"And yet you still doubt." He looked utterly per-plexed. "Do you not carry the brand of your Master?"

Brie nodded.

"Did you not vow to love him through better and worse?"

Her bottom lip quivered, but she nodded again.

"Whatever has you questioning that must be pro-found."

"It is."

"Then I suggest you hold on to what you know to be true."

"I will try."

"Succeeding is what Thane would expect."

Her voice faltered when she confessed, "The only time Sir has ever responded was when he smelled your cooking and Lilly spoke to him. It cuts me like a knife after everything I've tried."

He put his arms around her. "Thane is comforted by your presence. I am certain of it." He squeezed her even tighter, adding, "And who can blame the fellow for responding to my food?"

She chuckled softly, appreciating the comfort he provided.

"Let me take you home now. You can soak in a warm bath while I make you more soup."

Brie willing walked beside him down the hallway, but as they were waiting for the elevator she thought to herself, *If Sir is aware and if he is innocent, I can only imagine the hell he is going through stuck in a body that cannot respond to Lilly's betrayal—and my own doubts.*

"Master Anderson, I know this is a lot to ask, but can we stop by the hospital before we head home?"

He smiled down at her. "Now that's a request I would be honored to fulfill."

Brie was hopeful that on her return, she would feel differently toward Sir. However, once she was at his bedside, she found herself unsettled.

She knew the only thing Sir ever asked of her was to remain true to herself at all times. Keeping that in mind, she took his hand in hers. "Seeing Lilly pregnant with a baby she claims is yours has me questioning everything, Sir. Both Master Anderson and Mr. Thompson have advised me to keep my sights on what I know to be true. I am trying, Sir, I'm trying with all of my heart.

"But…" she said pleadingly, "I need a sign from you. Something—anything—to let me know you're here with me now."

She watched the monitor continue on as steady as ever. She then looked down at his hand in hers, thinking over and over again, *Squeeze it, Sir. Please just squeeze my hand.*

However, there was no movement, not even a twitch.

With a heavy heart, she lay his hand back on the bed cover and started to leave. She was about to walk through the door when she felt the overpowering urge to turn around.

When she did, her heart stopped.

Sir's eyes were open.

Master Anderson would never betray his friend, Thane Davis, but he would do almost anything for young Brie. Friendships will be tested in *A Cowboy's Heart*.

* I am switching things up, my friends! The next part of the journey is being told through Master Brad Anderson's POV.

Will the humorous Dom finally get his own happy ending?

Buy the next in the series:

#1 (Teach Me)

#2 (Love Me)

#3 (Catch Me)

#4 (Try Me)

#5 (Protect Me)

#6 (Hold Me)

#7 (Surprise Me)

#8 (Trust Me)

#9 (Claim Me)

#10 (Enchant Me)

#11 (A Cowboy's Heart)

You can also buy the Audio Book!

Enchant Me by **Red Phoenix**

Beautifully Narrated by Pippa Jayne

Enchant Me: Brie's Submission #10

Brie's Submission series:

Teach Me #1

Love Me #2

Catch Me #3

Try Me #4

Protect Me #5

Hold Me #6

Surprise Me #7

Trust Me #8

Claim Me #9

Enchant Me #10

A Cowboy's Heart #11

You can find Red on:
Twitter: @redphoenix69
Website: RedPhoenix69.com
Facebook: RedPhoenix69

 Keep up to date with the newest release of Brie by signing up for Red Phoenix's newsletter: redphoenix69.com/newsletter-signup

Red Phoenix is the author of:

Blissfully Undone
* Available in eBook and paperback
(Snowy Fun—Two people find themselves snowbound in a cabin where hidden love can flourish, taking one couple on a sensual journey into ménage à trois)

His Scottish Pet: Dom of the Ages
* Available in eBook and paperback
Audio Book: *His Scottish Pet: Dom of the Ages*
(Scottish Dom—A sexy Dom escapes to Scotland in the late 1400s. He encounters a waif who has the potential to free him from his tragic curse)

The Erotic Love Story of Amy and Troy
* Available in eBook and paperback
(Sexual Adventures—True love reigns, but fate continually throws Troy and Amy into the arms of others)

eBooks

Varick: The Reckoning

(Savory Vampire—A dark, sexy vampire story. The hero navigates the dangerous world he has been thrust into with lusty passion and a pure heart)

Keeper of the Wolf Clan (Keeper of Wolves, #1)

(Sexual Secrets—A virginal werewolf must act as the clan's mysterious Keeper)

The Keeper Finds Her Mate (Keeper of Wolves, #2)

(Second Chances—A young she-wolf must choose between old ties or new beginnings)

The Keeper Unites the Alphas (Keeper of Wolves, #3)

(Serious Consequences—The young she-wolf is captured by the rival clan)

Boxed Set: Keeper of Wolves Series (Books 1-3)

(Surprising Secrets—A secret so shocking it will rock Layla's world. The young she-wolf is put in a position of being able to save her werewolf clan or becoming the reason for its destruction)

Socrates Inspires Cherry to Blossom

(Satisfying Surrender—a mature and curvaceous woman becomes fascinated by an online Dom who has much to teach her)

By the Light of the Scottish Moon

(Saving Love—Two lost souls, the Moon, a werewolf and a death wish…)

In 9 Days

(Sweet Romance—A young girl falls in love with the new student, nicknamed 'the Freak')

---

9 Days and Counting

(Sacrificial Love—The sequel to In 9 Days delves into the emotional reunion of two longtime lovers)

And Then He Saved Me

(Saving Tenderness—When a young girl tries to kill herself, a man of great character intervenes with a love that heals)

Play With Me at Noon

(Seeking Fulfillment—A desperate wife lives out her fantasies by taking five different men in five days)

Connect with Red on Substance B

Substance B is a platform for independent authors to directly connect with their readers. Please visit Red's Substance B page where you can:

- Sign up for Red's newsletter
- Send a message to Red
- See all platforms where Red's books are sold

Visit Substance B today to learn more about your favorite independent authors.

CPSIA information can be obtained
at www.ICGtesting.com
Printed in the USA
LVOW01s1005120317
526915LV00008B/362/P